But Ms Brewster had not come alone. "Good morning, Harriet," Charlotte said briskly. "Apropos of our discussion, I've brought a possible client for your new venture. James Crawford—meet my accountant, Harriet Wilde."

Harriet got to her feet, feeling as though all the air had been sucked out of her office, as James, elegant in a dark City suit, strolled in and dominated it. After all the years of fantasising over a meeting here he was at last in the flesh: harder, older and colder, with little resemblance to the man she'd fallen in love with.

"Miss Wilde and I have already met," he informed Charlotte, the deep voice striking a chord so familiar Harriet's pulse went into overdrive as he held out his hand. He gave her a hard, bright look. "But it was so long ago you've probably forgotten."

"Of course not." She shook the hand, and felt a streak of heat along her veins at the contact.

Dear Reader

My life as a Jane Austen fan began when I was fourteen. Although a mere junior I won a role in the school production of *Pride and Prejudice* as the nasty Miss Bingley, decked out in a black velvet dress with my hair in ringlets.

I went on to read *Emma* and *Mansfield Park* in school, but I finally met up with *Persuasion* many years later when I was living in Brazil. I was confined to bed with a virus in the hottest part of the year, and was delighted when one of my husband's colleagues lent me selections from his library of classic literature, which included Dickens, the Brontes, Thomas Hardy and, most important of all, a large tome entitled *Jane Austen, The Works*. I devoured this from cover to cover, ending up with *Persuasion*, which was, and still is, my favourite of all Jane Austen's novels.

It was a challenge to achieve a modern romance based on the theme of Persuasion, with its codes of behaviour from a bygone age, but I hope you enjoy the final result as much as I enjoyed writing *A Wicked Persuasion*.

Love and best wishes,

Catherine

A WICKED PERSUASION

BY
CATHERINE GEORGE

MILLS & BOON

First published in Great Britain 2012
by Mills & Boon, an imprint of Harlequin (UK) Limited.
Harlequin (UK) Limited, Eton House, 18-24 Paradise Road,
Richmond, Surrey TW9 1SR

© Catherine George 2012

ISBN: 978 0 263 22680 5

Harlequin (UK) policy is to use papers that are natural, renewable and recyclable products and made from wood grown in sustainable forests. The logging and manufacturing process conform to the legal environmental regulations of the country of origin.

Printed and bound in Great Britain
by CPI Antony Rowe, Chippenham, Wiltshire

Catherine George was born in Wales, and early on developed a passion for reading which eventually fuelled her compulsion to write. Marriage to an engineer led to nine years in Brazil, but on his later travels the education of her son and daughter kept her in the UK. And, instead of constant reading to pass her lonely evenings, she began to write the first of her romantic novels. When not writing and reading, she loves to cook, listen to opera, and browse in antiques shops.

Recent titles by the same author:

UNDER THE BRAZILIAN SUN
THE POWER OF THE LEGENDARY GREEK
  (*Greek Tycoons*)
THE MISTRESS OF HIS MANOR
THE ITALIAN COUNT'S DEFIANT BRIDE
  (*International Billionaires*)

Did you know these are also available as eBooks?
Visit www.millsandboon.co.uk

With thanks to the immortal Jane

CHAPTER ONE

NOT a single thing had changed in the cobbled streets around the medieval market hall since the stormy day he'd driven away like a bat out of hell, swearing never to set foot in the place again. Ten years on, the steep roofs and stone mullions typical of local architecture glowed in the sun as he left the town centre for Broad Street to walk past graceful old buildings, the private dwellings outnumbered by medical consultants, banks, chartered accountants, solicitors and even interior designers. To satisfy his curiosity he went inside the bank he was aiming for and learned that one thing *had* changed. But on his way out he heard a voice behind him exchanging greetings with one of the bank clerks and stopped dead, his heart slamming rabbit punches against his ribs. He turned slowly, and felt a jolt of visceral satisfaction when the woman walking towards him turned so deathly pale he almost put out a hand to steady her.

'James!' She swallowed, so visibly shocked his satisfaction doubled as he held the door open for her.

'Why, hello! How are you, Harriet?' he asked affably.

'Very well.' A statement which was such a palpable lie he almost laughed in her face. 'And you?'

'Never better.' He glanced at his watch. 'Good to see you again, but I can't stop—running late. Goodbye.'

James Crawford strode down the street without a backward glance, angry because the chance sighting of Harriet Wilde had affected him so violently. She'd changed out of all recognition from the girl he'd once adored. The girl who'd shut him out of her life and changed his own for ever.

Harriet stood transfixed outside the bank, staring at the man striding away down the hill. At last she let out the breath she'd been holding and turned, shaken, to make for her car. For years after the painful break up she had dreamed of meeting James Crawford again. The result had been too many sleepless nights, and weight loss that ruined her looks, according to the siblings who'd accused her of dieting. And in time she had stopped imagining that every tall, dark male figure she spotted in the distance was James, mainly because in ten long years she had never actually laid eyes on him again. And now she had at last bumped into him, fate arranged it to be after a hard day's work when she probably looked every minute of the ten years since their last meeting. She hadn't bothered with lipstick since lunch, either. She smiled bitterly. It would take a lot more than lipstick to mend fences with James Crawford. Who was sure to be a husband and father long since. Harriet's sharp twinge of pain at the thought was the last straw. She'd been so sure she felt nothing for him any more. But it was only natural to feel *something*, if only to wonder what he was doing here after all this time. Her phone rang as she turned up the steep, winding drive but she let her father's call go to message. After the devastating encounter with James she was in sore need of some peace at her own place before tackling the evening ahead.

When Harriet had qualified as a chartered accountant she accepted a job with a local firm instead of a tempting offer from a London-based company, and then astonished her family by announcing that she wanted to move permanently into the Lodge at River House.

'Why on earth would you want to do that?' had demanded Julia, the eldest of the three Wilde sisters. 'It's so small!'

It was also self-contained, enough distance from the main house for privacy, but near enough to keep a monitoring eye on it. 'I like it there,' Harriet had told her. 'I've always used the Lodge to study, anyway. It's surely not unreasonable at my age to want a place of my own.'

Aubrey Wilde had dismissed the idea instantly. 'Don't be ridiculous. Why live down there alone?'

Because it would be infinitely preferable to life alone with him at the main house. Julia, the brilliant one, edited a fashion magazine in London, and rarely made time to come back to River House. Neither did the prettier, but considerably less brilliant Sophie, who was too involved with her child and husband, and her social life in Pennington.

'If you don't agree, Father, I'll get a flat in the town,' had been Harriet's impassive response. And because she was the daughter who did everything by the book, other than one teenage episode he preferred to forget ever happened, Aubrey Wilde had reluctantly agreed.

It would be a fight to get his agreement tonight. Harriet's mouth tightened as she wriggled into her favourite dress for morale. As a further boost she released her hair from its severe daytime coil and went to work with a brush. She alone had inherited her mother's abundant curling mane, and it gave Harriet a kick to know that envious Sophie had to resort to hair extensions and hours at the hairdresser to achieve anything remotely similar. Julia, of course, wore her black locks in a sleek crop that looked as if it cost a fortune to maintain and probably did. Harriet took a few seconds to slap on some make-up, slid on her tallest heels and, feeling about as happy as Daniel on the way to the lion's den, walked up the steep, winding drive to the house.

When Harriet entered the beloved old house via the back door a mouth-watering aroma scented the vast kitchen, but otherwise it was deserted. No surprise there. From the animated conversation coming from the drawing room along the hall, her siblings were enjoying pre-dinner drinks with their father, with no thought about the dinner itself. Julia and Sophie expected meals to appear without their assistance and, as she did on a regular basis, Harriet gave fervent thanks to the paragon who kept River House in perfect order. Margaret Rogers came in for three hours daily during the week to keep the house immaculate, supplied Aubrey Wilde with a light lunch when required, and stocked his freezer with dinners suitable to heat in the microwave she'd taught him to use. Consequently, he liked to boast that he was self-sufficient. But the actual yoke of householder lay light on his shoulders. Since his early retirement from the bank, Aubrey Wilde spent most of his time on the golf course, in the bar at its club, or at functions and dinners of various kinds.

Harriet checked the fragrant venison casserole keeping hot in the warming oven, then took the first course to the dining room. Julia, tall, faultlessly groomed and commanding, swept in while Harriet was setting out individual salads at one end of the long table she'd laid ready the night before.

'So there you are at last,' Julia said tartly. 'Pa's been trying to ring you.'

Harriet kissed the air near the expertly tinted cheek she was offered. 'My last client ran on a bit; I was late leaving the office.'

'While I've come all the way from London, and missed a very important meeting to get here,' Julia reminded her.

Harriet raised a cynical eyebrow. 'And spent the entire train journey on the phone, harassing your underlings.'

Julia made no attempt to deny it. 'So what's the big mystery? Why are two or three of us gathered together? It can't be to pray.'

'It might come to that. I need your backup tonight.'

'That's new.' Julia's eyes narrowed. 'You're not involved with someone unsuitable again by any chance?'

Harriet gave her a withering look and turned to make for the kitchen.

'I'll report back to Father that you've arrived,' called her sister. 'Want a drink?'

'Not yet, thanks.' Harriet was well aware that her fashion guru sister was inspecting her rear view in the clinging dress. Not that she cared. Some of the weight she'd lost over James had been regained eventually, but she was still a dress size smaller than Julia and at least two less than Sophie.

Harriet's lips tightened as she put asparagus to steam. After years of absence from her life, it was the second intrusion of the day by James Crawford, the 'someone unsuitable' in her past. A mere technician with a computer firm had been dismissed as totally out of the question for a daughter of River House. And, to Harriet's despair, her godmother, who until that point had been her constant ally, had agreed with Aubrey Wilde for the first time in living memory.

'Darling, you're too young,' Miriam Cairns had told her. 'You're doing too well at university to get serious with anyone. If this young man is as wonderful as you say he'll wait until you're qualified.'

But James, unwilling to wait, had persuaded Harriet to share a flat with him near the college while she finished her course.

When Aubrey Wilde learned of the plan he'd lost his temper completely. Crimson with fury, he'd roared that he would get the director of the computer firm, a golfing crony of his, to fire his employee immediately. And if Harriet persisted in her defiance a restraining order would be taken out against the upstart, which would mean arrest if the man dared to come anywhere near Miss Harriet Wilde again. Appalled, she had argued long and passionately, and in desperation finally resorted to pleading. But her incensed father had remained immovable. In the end Harriet had given in, afraid that if she continued to defy him Aubrey Wilde would carry out his threat.

Harriet had been forced to tell James that living with him while she was still studying was not possible. 'With you around to distract me I would never qualify.'

At first James had laughed, sure she was joking, but when he saw she was in deadly earnest he had done his utmost to change her mind until at last he threw up his hands in angry defeat. 'So that's it?' he said at last, his voice rough with emotion. 'On your bike, Crawford, and never darken my door again.'

'Of course not,' she said in misery, tears running down her face. 'Things will be different once I'm qualified—'

'You actually expect me to be fool enough to hang around that long, Harriet?' His sarcastic smile cut her to pieces. 'Daddy said no, didn't he? And like a good little daughter you're giving in without a fight.'

'I had no *choice*,' she said brokenly.

'There's always a choice!' His eyes glittered with rage and bitter hurt. 'But you've obviously made yours, little girl. So get lost. Run home to Daddy and grow up.'

Harriet had rung him the moment she got home, and sobbed in utter despair when she found his phone had been disconnected and his email wiped. James Crawford, the computer expert, had cut off all means of communication. After a sleepless night, she went to his lodgings first thing next morning, to find that he had already paid up and left. And until that brief encounter today she had never seen him again.

The oven timer went off, jerking Harriet back from the past. She loaded the trolley and trundled it along to the dining room, then joined the others to say that dinner was served.

'About time,' complained Sophie, jumping up. 'I'm starving.'

'But as usual it never occurred to you to lend a hand,' said Harriet, with a sharpness so unlike her the other three stared, taken aback.

'Busy day?' asked her father warily.

Sophie bridled, flushing. 'I've been busy too, I'd have you know. Annabel runs me ragged.'

'Really? I thought she ran your wonderful Pilar ragged,' said Harriet, referring to Sophie's au pair, and Julia laughed.

'Got you there, Sophie.'

Aubrey Wilde eyed Harriet uneasily. 'Something wrong?'

'No more than usual,' she said tersely. 'Let's eat before poor little Sophie fades away from malnutrition.'

Sophie, who was anything but little, opened her mouth to snap back a furious retort, but caught her father's quelling eye and subsided, sulking, as they took their places in the dining room. Harriet was glad of the wine her father poured for her, but the ordeal looming after the meal killed her enthusiasm for the perfect little salads. To her surprise, Julia carried the used dishes to a sideboard afterwards and ordered Sophie to hand round plates as Harriet served the venison, while Aubrey watched benignly, delighted to see his daughters working in such accord.

'So why did you want us here tonight, Daddy?' asked Sophie when they were back in the drawing room.

'Nothing to do with me.' He shrugged, and poured himself a cognac. 'Splendid as it is to have all my girls with me, it's Harriet's idea, not mine.'

Julia raised her perfectly threaded eyebrows at her sister. 'Please tell me I haven't forgotten some occasion of significance, Harriet. At least I know it's not your birthday. Have you had a promotion?'

'Sadly, no.' Harriet produced her briefcase.

'Oh, bother,' groaned Sophie. 'Don't say we have to sign things.'

'No, you don't.' Harriet drew up a low table, and spread out some documents. 'But it's important that you and Julia are present at this discussion.'

Her father glared at her. 'Harriet, if this is about accounts you should have discussed it with me first!'

'In which case,' she said without emotion, 'you know perfectly well you would have dismissed my findings as pessimistic nonsense.'

Sophie burst into indignant protest, but Julia silenced her with an upraised hand. 'These are the accounts for the financial year, Harriet?'

'Yes.' For once Harriet was glad of Julia's input. 'I may not have spoken to Father first tonight, but I assure you I've tried to reason with him on countless other nights before finally calling you both in.'

Aubrey reddened. 'The girl's always hammering at me to retrench. But dammit, I lead a very simple life since I retired. How can I be expected to cut down any further?'

Harriet went in for the kill. 'You sell the house, Father.'

For once Julia and Sophie were in accord as they looked from Harriet to their father in utter horror.

'Sell River House?' gasped Sophie.

Julia frowned. 'It's as bad as that?'

Harriet eyed her father in challenge, and with much throat clearing he finally admitted that his finances were in a bad way. 'Like a good many other people, I took a beating on the market recently,' he admitted gruffly, and poured another brandy.

'And the bottom line, Harriet?' demanded Julia.

'As things stand, Father can't afford to go on living here without extra revenue coming in. This is a high maintenance house.'

Aubrey nodded morosely. 'In your grandfather's day there was a builder on call, and two full-time gardeners on the payroll. Now I get Ed Haines in for maintenance only when strictly necessary, and his son for one day a week in the garden.'

'And you're rapidly running out of funds for even that much,' said Harriet with finality.

Sophie turned on her angrily. 'Are you sure you've got this right? Shouldn't one of the senior partners in your firm be doing Father's accounts, not someone junior like you?'

Aubrey Wilde eyed her in disapproval. 'Apologise to Harriet at once, Sophie.'

'Sorry, sorry!' Sophie burst into noisy tears. 'But I just can't bear the thought of River House being sold.'

'Since Harriet is a qualified chartered accountant,' snapped Julia who, if not affectionate, was always just, 'her figures are obviously correct.'

'They were checked by one of the senior partners. Rex Barlow went over them with me, at my request, and agreed with me on every count,' said Harriet wearily. 'Funds are needed urgently, or Father has no option. He must sell up.'

'I can't manage anything significant in the way of financial help,' said Julia with regret. 'The mortgage on the new flat is a killer.'

'And I can't ask Gervase for money!' said Sophie in alarm. 'He was absolutely horrid to me about my last credit card bill.'

'Even if either of you could contribute something it would just be a temporary stopgap. However—' Harriet paused, almost amused as the other three regarded her in sudden hope '—if you can't bear the thought of selling, Father, there might just possibly be another way round the problem.'

He brightened. 'You've thought of something?'

'Can't you pay Father more rent for the Lodge?' said Sophie.

'If you can't say anything sensible, for God's sake keep quiet,' snapped Julia. 'Just for the record, how much do you pay, Harriet?'

Colour rose again in Aubrey's face when Harriet told her.

'I know it's too much—'

'Far too much,' said Julia trenchantly. 'No one else would pay anything like that to live in such a poky little place—not that you haven't made it charming, Harriet,' she added fairly, 'and entirely at your own expense at that. But you know damn well you could rent a luxury flat in the town for that money.'

'So why do you stay here then?' muttered Sophie sulkily.

'Because if River House is to remain in the family it needs constant care,' Harriet told her flatly. 'When I qualified I offered my free professional help to Father, which means I do the accounts, make sure the household bills are paid on time and consult regularly with Ed Haines about basic house maintenance. But if something isn't done soon, there won't be enough money even for that. You'll have to let Margaret Rogers go, Father, and do the housework and gardening yourself. And sell the new car,' she added ruthlessly.

This last was so obviously the last straw it would have been amusing in any other circumstances. 'So what do you have in mind?' he asked, with unusual humility.

'Charlotte Brewster is the client who made me late today.'

'The one who was Head Girl in my day?' said Julia with interest.

Harriet nodded. 'She chose me as her accountant because of the school connection.'

'Never mind all that,' said Aubrey impatiently. 'What has this woman to do with our problem?'

'She's a professional location agent, working with people who hire out their houses as venues for films, PR events, commercial photo shoots, and so on,' Harriet told him, human enough to feel satisfaction when his jaw dropped.

'You're actually suggesting I let a film crew stampede all over my home?' he said, aghast.

'If they find it suitable for their purposes, yes.'

Sophie's eyes shone. 'How exciting!'

Julia eyed Harriet with respect. 'Actually it's a brilliant idea. You can charge big bucks for just a day's filming. And I *can* be of help in this way. I could get my people to do a shoot here, put out feelers in other directions, too.'

'Great idea.' Harriet turned back to her father. 'Of course, as an alternative, you could stay with Miriam and let the entire house out for the summer.'

'God forbid,' he said in horror. 'Miriam and I would kill each other in days.'

'Then you have no option,' said Harriet briskly. 'I can take a room in town while the house is in use, and you can move into the Lodge, Father.'

Julia nodded thoughtfully. 'The gardens alone would

be a huge draw. Dress designers would salivate over this place—models gazing through the wisteria on the veranda, or draped over the balcony outside my bedroom.'

'And mine,' echoed Sophie.

Harriet looked at her father. 'So what's your answer?'

His mouth twisted. 'You've already decided for me.'

'Shall I put the idea to the vote?'

'Unnecessary,' said Julia crisply. 'It's a three to one majority.'

Her father sighed, defeated. 'Oh, very well, I'll make it unanimous, but on condition that when these people rampage over the house *you* stay in the Lodge to keep an eye on them, Harriet. I'll find somewhere in town. And now, Sophie,' he added in a different tone, 'I suggest you help Julia clear the dining room and load the dishwasher.' He waited until they left the room, then turned to Harriet. 'You really think this will work?'

She nodded. 'It must work. The roof is the top priority. I checked with Ed.'

'Why not with me?'

'Because you turn a blind eye to what you don't want to see!'

He sighed. 'You've changed such a lot, Harriet.'

She shook her head. 'You just haven't noticed before.'

'I notice more than you realise,' he said bleakly, 'including why you refuse to live here at home with me.'

Harriet was relieved when her sisters' reappearance put a welcome end to the tense silence which followed her father's statement. Soon afterwards, Sophie drove home, and Harriet retreated thankfully to the Lodge without mentioning that someone was already interested in taking River House over for a project. It had seemed best to get her father used to the idea before hitting him with the first punter right away.

But instead of concentrating on a workable solution to the problem of River House's finances, Harriet's mind kept returning to the past once she was in bed. Over the years she had trained herself to forget that James Crawford existed, but running into him earlier had brought back that long ago idyllic summer so vividly that sleep was impossible.

The Lodge, once occupied by Margaret before her marriage to John Rogers, had been empty when Harriet announced at fifteen that she wanted to take it over to study there in peace. In return for her father's permission she'd promised to take care of it herself. She was at her desk there one hot summer morning a few years later when her computer crashed. A frantic phone call to the local suppliers brought quick response in the shape of a tall young technician with shaggy black hair and bright hazel eyes which lit up with gratifying pleasure at the sight of her.

'Hi. I'm from Combe Computers,' he said in deep gravel tones which sent shivers down her spine.

Harriet smiled shyly and showed him into the small sitting room she'd made into a study. She gestured to the computer on the desk. 'Can you do anything with it?'

'I'll do my best, Miss Wilde.'

'Harriet.'

'James.' He smiled. 'James Crawford.'

She curled up on the window seat to watch as he set to work, impressed by his skill as he took the machine apart.

'It's the mother board,' he announced after a while, and opened his bulging black bag. 'I'll fit a new one. It won't take long.'

He was right. Far too soon for Harriet, the computer was up and running and James Crawford was ready to leave.

'I can't thank you enough,' she said warmly as she saw

him to the door. 'I was tearing my hair out before you came.'

'A crime with hair like yours!' He smiled down at her in the tiny porch. 'Do you work in the evenings, too?'

'Sometimes.'

'How about taking time off to come out for a drink tonight?'

'Yes,' she said promptly.

His smile sent her brain reeling. 'I like a woman who knows her own mind. I'll pick you up at seven.'

'No, thanks,' she said hastily. 'I'll meet you. Where?'

From that first night in a small pub far enough from the town to give them anonymity, they'd found an immediate rapport. Unknown to Aubrey Wilde and Miriam Cairns, or to Sophie, who was away in France for the summer with her best friend's family, they spent every moment possible together from that night on. If questioned on her whereabouts, Harriet enlisted the willing help of a friend, and lied shamelessly that she was making the most of her time with Anne during her vacation. As the time drew near for Harriet to leave for her second year at university the prospect of parting grew so painful James came up with the idea of sharing a flat near the college for the duration of her course.

'I can freelance, and still be on call for the firm,' he assured her. 'Most important of all, we can be together.'

Harriet had agreed rapturously, willing to defy her father on her own account when it came to living with the man she loved, but in the end afraid to risk ruin to James Crawford's career when Aubrey Wilde's threats sounded the death knell to the plan.

CHAPTER TWO

HARRIET woke next morning with dark-ringed eyes which needed serious work with camouflage before she was ready to face her day. To her surprise, Julia arrived as she was about to leave. 'I thought you were having a lie-in!'

Julia nodded glumly. 'So did I. But my body clock is still ticking on London time. Besides, I wanted to catch you before you took off. Does Charlotte Brewster already have something in mind for River House? Knowing you, cautious one, I was pretty sure you wouldn't have stated your case so strongly otherwise.'

'You're right. She's sending me our first punter this morning. Some man who wants the house for a party.' Harriet looked at her watch. 'I'd better get going. I'll give you a ring tonight to report.'

'In that case I'll be noble and keep Sophie in the loop for you.' Julia shot her sister a wry look. 'I suppose you know why she's such a cow to you?'

Harriet nodded. 'She's jealous of my so-called relationship with Father.'

Julia eyed her thoughtfully. 'She hasn't a clue, has she? So why do you stay?'

Harriet concentrated on packing her briefcase. 'Because just before…before the end, I promised Mother I would help Father take good care of River House.'

Julia shook her head in disapproval. 'Leave him to do it himself. I love the place too, but you need more in your life than a house, Harriet! Mother would be the first to agree with me.'

'I enjoy a normal social life,' said Harriet defensively.

'Ah, but do you ever enjoy a sleepover with the men you go out with? I doubt that you ask anyone back here!'

'For heaven's sake, Julia, it's too early in the morning for this—I have to go.'

Julia paused in the doorway. 'Take my advice—if money does come in this way, or any other way at all, get part of it tied up tight in a separate business account for the house. Otherwise Pa might start dabbling in shares and Lord knows what else again and we'll be back to square one.'

'I intend to,' Harriet assured her. 'When I break the glad news to him can I say I have your full support?'

'Absolutely. Good luck.'

Harriet reached the premises in Broad Street on time, as usual. She exchanged greetings with Lydia, the long-time receptionist, and made for the small office with a single tall window overlooking the gardens—a view that more than compensated for lack of space. As she gazed out for her brief morning ritual of peace, the new trainee came in to ask about coffee.

'Not right now, thanks, Simon.' Harriet smiled at him. 'Bring some when my nine-thirty appointment arrives. Tell Lydia to buzz you the moment he does so you can usher him in with due pomp.'

'Will do. You look good today,' he remarked. 'New suit?'

'New to you, yes.' She smiled. 'Now, hop off and let me get on.'

Harriet worked steadily for an hour before taking a break

to tidy up. She was back at her desk, absorbed again, when Simon knocked on her door and ushered in her client.

'Your nine-thirty appointment, Miss Wilde,' he announced.

Harriet got to her feet feeling as though all the air had been sucked out of her office as James Crawford, elegant in a dark city suit, strolled in and dominated it by the sheer force of his personality. Now she had the time to take a good look, she could see that he was harder, older and colder, with little resemblance to the man she'd fallen in love with.

'Good morning, Harriet.' He held out his hand. 'I had no time yesterday to mention we'd be meeting in an official capacity today.'

Or he wanted to give her a nasty surprise. 'Good morning.' Manfully hiding her shock, Harriet took the strong, slim hand. Ignoring the searing streak of heat along her veins at the contact, she smiled politely. 'This is a surprise. Charlotte Brewster told me I had a possible client to hire River House, but she forgot to give me a name.'

James drew up a chair in front of her desk and sat down, looking so relaxed Harriet wanted to hit him. 'She didn't forget. I asked to remain anonymous.'

'Why?'

His eyes gleamed with mockery. 'In case you refused to see me.'

'Why would I do that?' she said, determinedly pleasant.

Simon came in bearing a tray with the silver coffee pot and fine china normally reserved for clients of the senior partner. 'Ring if you need anything else, Miss Wilde.'

'Thank you, Simon.'

Once she'd served James's coffee, Harriet forced herself to sip hers slowly rather than glug the caffeine down like medicine.

'To business,' said James briskly, putting his cup down. 'I met Ms Brewster over the weekend. During our conversation I told her I believe in keeping my employees happy and was on the lookout for an unusual location to throw a party for them.' His eyes speared hers. 'Imagine my surprise when she suggested River House.'

She could, vividly. 'What kind of company do you run?'

'We provide broadband and phone lines to businesses and various commercial outfits,' he informed her, and smiled. 'I've moved on a bit from the day I was called out to repair your computer. The usual rags-to-riches story, according to the press.'

'Congratulations. I'm afraid I missed reading about it.' She glued her smile in place. 'So what, exactly, did you have in mind with regard to River House?' Other than humiliating Harriet Wilde by hiring her home.

He leaned back, still irritatingly relaxed. 'Briefly, my aim is a party to celebrate the recent expansion in my Live Wires Group. I've recently taken over a couple of small companies who ran into trouble. This event will welcome their employees on to my staff, and at the same time reward my original workforce for their efforts. I could use a hotel, obviously, but I liked the idea of an actual home setting as a venue.'

The Wilde home in particular. 'River House doesn't have room to put many people up overnight,' Harriet warned, her mind in turmoil behind her professional demeanour.

He shook his head. 'Not my intention. Transport will be provided for arrival and departure on the same day. I seem to remember a terrace leading to a large lawn, so a marquee seems the most practical idea, with drinks on the terrace beforehand if the weather's good. What parking facilities can you provide?'

'There's an adjoining paddock we used for my sister's

wedding. Would your caterers need the kitchen?' By this stage Harriet was experiencing serious qualms about hiring her home to any client, let alone to James Crawford.

'The firm I have in mind provides their own,' he informed her. 'And the other necessary facilities will be set up out of sight somewhere in the gardens. You need suffer very little intrusion on your privacy.'

Harriet smiled coolly. 'It makes no difference to me personally. I don't live there.'

He tensed, eyes narrowed. 'You're based here in the town?'

'No. Perhaps you may remember the Lodge at River House? I've lived there for quite a while.'

Of course he remembered the Lodge! James tried to look as though he were attempting to recall it. 'I see.' But he didn't. This self-contained woman with her tailored suit and severe, pulled back hair was very different from the warm, loving girl he remembered. But then, when push came to shove that girl had not cared enough for him to give up her lifestyle at River House. For which he should be eternally grateful. The hurt and humiliation she'd dished out had fired him with the ambition to make such a success of his life James Crawford would be good enough for anyone, Aubrey Wilde's daughter included. It was a blow to hear she'd moved out of River House itself, but if her father still lived there that would have to do.

'I'll need to see over the house,' he informed her, 'at some time convenient to you and your father, of course.'

Of course. Harriet had been steeling herself for that from the moment he entered her office and turned her life on its head again.

'I'm staying in the locality with my sister for a few days,' said James, 'so any time up to, and including, Sunday would suit me.'

'Perhaps I could ring you later when I've had a word with my father.'

'By all means.' James stood up and handed her a card. 'You can reach me on any of the numbers. Goodbye…Miss Wilde.' He strode from her office and down the hall, smiling briefly at the receptionist as he said goodbye. Outside in bright morning sunshine he breathed in deeply, savouring the overwhelming satisfaction of the moment. It had taken a long time and a hell of a lot of hard graft to achieve financial success, while George Lassiter, his old boss, had hinted over lunch recently that Aubrey Wilde's finances were not too buoyant these days. James's eyes glittered coldly. They must be reaching crisis point if he was willing to hire his house out to the man who'd once been considered unfit to enter its hallowed portals.

As soon as she heard the street door close Harriet rang Charlotte Brewster to report.

'James said he knew you slightly years ago and asked to remain anonymous so he could surprise you,' Charlotte informed her. 'How well *did* you know him?'

'When I was a student he came to the Lodge to mend my computer. But before I let James Crawford look over River House, Ms Brewster, I need to know how much he's willing to pay for the privilege.'

Charlotte chuckled. 'You sounded just like Julia then! When I was a prefect we clashed constantly. I hear she edits one of those glossy style magazines these days. Did she marry?'

'Not yet.'

'And you're not married either—though the love of your life is easy to identify!'

Harriet went cold.

'River House obviously means the world to you,'

Charlotte continued with sympathy. 'But take my advice; don't expend all your love on bricks and mortar. A man in one's life is no bad thing, you know.'

'Fascinating though the subject is, Charlotte, let's get down to brass tacks. How much will Mr Crawford cough up to hire River House?'

Harriet drove home in a very different mood from the night before. One detail apart, she had good news for her father. By the time she reached the Lodge she had even recovered enough from the shock of James Crawford as their first client to enjoy a solitary, celebratory meal alone before she went up to the house. She found her father hovering in the kitchen, waiting for her.

'Well?' he said eagerly. 'Julia said you were seeing this Brewster woman today. Do you have good news?'

'Yes. Let's discuss it over coffee in the study.'

'I've already made it for you,' he said, surprising her.

Once they were settled in the study Harriet informed him that her meeting had been with an actual client for the new venture, and told him how much the client would pay for hiring River House to host a party for his workforce. 'But this is where I burst your bubble, Father.'

He was thinking with such rapture of the fee he took time to register her remark. 'Eh? What's that?'

'To make this arrangement work, only part of the money will be paid into your personal account; the rest will go into a business account only I will draw on for maintenance for River House. Julia is in full agreement with me on this.' Harriet's eyes locked with his, and Aubrey Wilde nodded, defeated.

'Whatever you say. But it's a sad day when daughters don't trust their father.'

Not without cause, thought Harriet, unmoved. 'Charlotte

Brewster tells me she has several further possibilities in mind for River House, so our venture has every chance of being successful. On condition, she emphasizes, that the house and gardens are maintained to a standard high enough to attract future clients.'

Aubrey raised his still handsome head, his smile bleak. 'I hear you. I'll sign on whatever dotted line you put in front of me—once I've read every word of the small print, of course.'

'Of course,' she agreed, relaxing slightly.

'This would be damned embarrassing if I were still at the bank. I'm glad I retired when I did,' he said, depressed.

'Yet you of all people know that a business account like this makes sense,' said Harriet briskly, watching closely while he signed the documents. 'By the way, the client would like to see over the house and garden as soon as possible. Do you want to be here when he comes?'

He looked up irritably. 'Of course I do! Dammit, girl, it's my home! Just make sure you're here, too.'

'As you wish. I'd rather not take time off so I'll suggest Saturday to the client and ask Will to give us extra time in the garden beforehand. The weather forecast is good for the weekend, fortunately. I checked.'

He nodded glumly. 'Saturday it is then. I was booked to play golf, but I'll cancel.'

'Good. I'll ask the client to come at ten.'

'Who is he, by the way?'

'Head of the Live Wires Group.'

'Can't say I've heard of it. But it must be successful if he's prepared to shell out like this just to entertain his employees. You'd better have a word with Mrs Rogers to prepare her, Harriet.'

'It won't affect her too much. Margaret keeps the entire

house at inspection standard all the time anyway. And the kitchen won't be needed for the party catering.'

'But people will be swarming all over the rest of the house,' he said gloomily.

'Not in this instance. There's to be a marquee on the lawn—probably like the one you had for Sophie's wedding.'

'The affair won't be too intrusive then.' Aubrey hovered as she packed the documents away. 'If that's everything I might as well go out for an hour.'

'Cheer up, Father. It's better than selling the house.'

'By God you're right,' he said with feeling, and squeezed her hand. 'You're a good girl, Harriet.'

She withdrew her hand gently. 'Goodnight, Father.'

Harriet returned to the Lodge and stood at the window, watching her father's newest car purr down the drive. She left a message for Julia to report on the meeting, and finally steeled herself to contact James.

'This is Harriet—Harriet Wilde.'

'I haven't forgotten your name! So when do we meet?'

'Does Saturday suit you?'

'Saturday is fine to inspect the house, but I need to see you before then, Harriet. Or should I keep to Miss Wilde?'

She stiffened. 'Your choice entirely. Why do you want to see me?'

'There are some points I'd like to go over with you before I meet up with your father.'

His money is getting us out of a hole, she reminded herself. 'When would you like to come to my office?'

'I meant a private meeting—over dinner tomorrow evening.'

Harriet almost dropped her phone. 'Is that absolutely necessary?'

'Imperative. I need certain facts clarified before I come to River House. Don't worry,' he added sardonically, 'I'm not asking to dine *à deux*. I'm staying with my sister. The dinner invitation is from Moira.'

Harriet's eyebrows rose. 'How very kind of her.'

'You'll come then?'

Think of the money, she chanted in a silent mantra. 'Where does your sister live?'

'A couple of miles off the Oxford road as you leave town. Her husband recently bought The Old Rectory at Wood End. I'll pick you up at seven thirty.'

'No—thank you,' she said quickly. 'I'm sure I can find it.'

Harriet felt oddly baffled as she disconnected. James could hardly intend to taunt her about the past at his sister's dinner table. Hiring River House would surely be revenge enough for him without that. But for a split second at the office she could have sworn he'd been ready to change his mind when he heard she no longer lived in the house. But surely he would have said he intended backing out while he was in her office, rather than have his sister invite her to dinner. Moira Crawford, Harriet knew, had stood in *loco parentis* to James and his brother after their parents died, and made a good job of it by the affection in his voice when he spoke of her. It was a surprise to learn that she lived locally now.

James, she thought, depressed, had changed out of all recognition from the charmer she'd fallen in love with. At one time the gravel tones in his voice had rendered her weak at the knees, but during the interview they had acted like sandpaper on her nerves. His hair was more disciplined and the lanky body had gained muscle and hardened, and his dress sense was now impeccable, all as she would have expected. His personality was the big difference. She had adored his smile in the old days, but there'd been no sign of it today. The driving ambition necessary to build up a successful telecom company obviously left no room for the soft option of charm.

Harriet made sure she finished work on the dot the following day, in good time to prepare herself for crossing swords with the client who had once been her sweetheart. But never her actual lover. Knowing he would be her first, he'd indulged her plea to wait until they moved in together. Which, looking back, would have been a recipe for disaster. With James sharing her bed it would have been a wrench to leave it to attend lectures. Even so, if she had been the sole target of her father's anger she would have dug her heels in and defied him. But his threat to have James arrested had beaten her into the dust.

Harriet thrust thoughts of the past away as she dealt with her exuberant hair, which was neither dark like Julia's nor fair like Sophie's, but a shade somewhere between. When it was restrained in the workaday coil it looked quite dark, but newly washed and let loose on her shoulders it took on light and shade and transformed her appearance, as she well knew. She shrugged. It was only common sense to face James armed with the best weapon in her armoury. She tugged on the clinging black dress, hung gilt and crystal drops in her ears, and saw her father coming down the drive as she opened the door to leave.

'Ah,' he said, crestfallen, 'you're going out. Mrs Rogers left me so much food I hoped you might join me for dinner for once.'

'Sorry, Father,' she said politely. 'I'm having dinner with a friend.' Sort of.

It was a measure of their relationship these days that Aubrey Wilde didn't even ask the identity of the friend. 'Another time then, Harriet. Enjoy your evening.'

* * *

The Old Rectory at Wood End dated from the eighteen-hundreds, when families of the clergy were usually large. Harriet's eyes narrowed as she drove up the tree-lined drive towards the house. It looked more than big enough for a party. Her heart gave an errant thump when James appeared as she parked on the gravel circle in front of the main door.

He came to help her out of the car looking more like the young man she'd once known than the successful tycoon he'd become. His casual garb gave her a moment's doubt about her dress until she saw that his sweater was cashmere, and the jeans fitted his long legs so faithfully they'd obviously been cut by a master.

'Good evening, Harriet,' he said, his eyes on her hair.

She smiled at him serenely. 'Hi.' She looked up at the façade of windows as he led her to the door. 'What a lovely house.'

He turned to the woman hurrying to join them. 'My sister,' James informed his guest. 'Moira, this is Harriet Wilde.'

'Welcome, Harriet.' Moira smiled warmly as she took the sheaf of flowers her guest handed her. 'How lovely, thank you. Come on in. We're all out here. My husband will give you a drink while I see to the flowers.'

All? Harriet followed her hostess across a wide hall and into a conservatory looking out over the back garden. A large smiling man got to his feet, followed by two young women, one with opulent curves and sheets of straight blonde hair, the other a less spectacular brunette.

'Marcus Graveney,' said her host, shaking her hand. 'These are my stepsisters, Claudia and Lily.'

'Hi,' said the sultry Claudia without enthusiasm, leaving Lily to make up for it with the sincere warmth of her greeting.

Marcus gave Harriet the glass of tonic she chose, and

led her to one of the comfortable cane chairs. 'James says you're a native of these parts.'

She nodded. 'I'm an accountant with Barlow & Greer in the town.'

Claudia made a face. 'Isn't that deadly dull?'

'It would be for you,' said James indulgently.

'A closer relationship with figures wouldn't do you any harm, Miss, dull or not,' said her brother.

'Do you enjoy your job?' asked Lily.

'Yes,' said Harriet with truth. 'It's a very busy practice, and I meet a lot of interesting people in the course of my work.'

'It's good of you to spare the time to come this evening,' said James as he sat down next to Claudia.

'I often dine with clients as part of the job,' Harriet assured him.

'Surely you're not going to talk business over dinner, James,' said Claudia, pouting.

'Not over the meal.' He slid a consoling arm round her waist. 'I'll borrow your study for a few moments afterwards if I may, Marcus. Harriet and I can have our talk in there without boring your sisters.'

Moira Graveney was a cook of considerable skill, and in other circumstances Harriet would have enjoyed the meal and the lively conversation, during which she learned that Marcus had recently joined the legal chambers near her offices in Broad Street. But with James's arm brushing hers from time to time, and waves of hostility sizzling across the table from Claudia, it was a relief when Moira finally suggested they all adjourn to the conservatory for coffee.

'Harriet and I will have ours in the study, love,' said James.

'Thank you for a delicious meal, Mrs Graveney,' said

Harriet, surprised to see a look of sympathy in Moira's distinctive hazel eyes.

'Do call me Moira. But you weren't hungry, were you?'

'On a diet?' said Claudia sweetly.

'No. Just a bit tired.'

'Unlike some people, lazybones, Harriet's been slaving away all day,' said Lily in typical sister fashion. 'And you're the one on a diet—not that it's working.'

'Now then, girls,' said their brother, and waved them away. 'You carry on, James. I'll send coffee in for you.'

James led Harriet to a very masculine panelled room. 'This is Marcus's retreat, where sermons were written in the past. When they moved here shortly after their marriage earlier this year, a study was his top priority. Moira's was the large garden we never had when we were young.'

Harriet sat down in the big leather chair he held out for her and got to the point. 'So have you brought me in here to read me a sermon, James?'

He held up a hand and went to the door to let in Claudia with a tray. 'Thanks, sweetheart.'

She reached up and tapped his cheek with a red-tipped finger. 'Don't be long.'

Harriet smiled politely as James handed her a cup of coffee. 'Thank you. So what did you want to talk about?'

He sat behind the desk, the dark-rimmed hazel irises spearing hers. 'No sermon, but I want some information before I meet your father—for the first time, incidentally, even though he tried to get me sacked from Combe Computers. Does he know who he's dealing with?'

Harriet raised an eyebrow. 'Tried?'

He nodded. 'George Lassiter didn't actually sack me all those years ago, Harriet. He merely transferred me up to his Newcastle outfit, which got me far away from you, as your father wanted, but kept me very firmly on George's payroll. He even gave me a rise. I was really good at my job, remember. Or had you forgotten?'

'No. I hadn't forgotten.' Anything. She looked at him steadily. 'I haven't told my father who you are other than the client paying good money to hire River House for a party.'

He eyed her grimly. 'So when I introduce myself he might cancel the whole idea!'

Harriet shook her head. 'It's all signed and sealed. My father can't back out.' Nor would he if it meant losing such easy money.

'When Ms Brewster suggested River House as a location I thought I was hearing things.' James's smile sent shivers down her spine. 'It was just too good to pass up.'

'For payback?'

'What else?' He frowned. 'Yet you don't actually live in the house any more. What the devil are you doing alone at the Lodge?'

'I wanted a place of my own.'

'I can understand that, but if that was your goal why not live down in the town? Or couldn't you bear to be too far away from Daddy?' When she made no response to that he eyed her curiously. 'I thought you'd be married by now.'

'Ditto!'

He shook his head. 'After the treatment you dished out, Miss Wilde, I gave up on relationships and concentrated on the really important things in life—success and money.'

'With spectacular results. I congratulate you.' She stood up. 'If that's all you wanted I'll go home now, and let you get back to Claudia.'

He laughed. 'She's jealous as hell of you, Harriet.'

She eyed him blankly. 'Really? Why?'

'I told her that you and I had a fling together once upon a time.'

'A fling?' she said with distaste.

He raised a mocking eyebrow. 'How else would you describe something so unimportant?'

She dropped her eyes. 'I never thought of it that way.'

'I'm surprised you ever thought of it at all!' he said caustically.

'Are you?' She looked at her watch. 'I really must go. Does ten on Saturday work for you?'

'Perfectly.' He opened the door for her.

Harriet caught a whiff of soap and expensive wool as she passed him; and something else that was so familiar and singularly James she felt dizzy.

'Hey,' he said quickly, 'are you all right?'

She forced a smile. 'Too much coffee, and too many late nights.'

'You're as white as a sheet,' he said roughly. 'Let me drive you home. I'll get your car back to you tomorrow.'

'No! Please, I'm fine. I just need to get to bed.' And, please God, sleep when she got there.

James eyed her closely as they made for the conservatory. 'You obviously work too hard,' he said, the familiar husky tone in his voice more pronounced. 'No change there; you always did, even as a teenager.'

Moira got up with a welcoming smile as they joined the others. 'You weren't long.'

'Mission accomplished,' said Harriet, and returned the smile warmly. 'It's been such a pleasure to meet you. Thank you again for the delicious dinner.'

Moira's face fell. 'Surely you're not leaving already, dear? It's early, and I've had no chance to talk to you!'

Marcus came to stand by his wife. 'They obviously work you too hard at your firm, Harriet.'

From the look on Claudia's face, this plainly meant she

looked like a hag. Harriet smiled brightly. 'It's a busy time right now.'

'It's been lovely to meet you. Please come again,' said Lily eagerly. 'We don't know anyone here.'

'And never likely to out in the wilds like this,' complained her sister, and pouted at Marcus. 'All right for you newly-weds, but not much fun for us.'

He gave her a quelling look and put an arm round his wife. 'Since you city girls only come here on flying visits it's hardly a problem.'

Time to go, thought Harriet. I get enough angst with my own family. 'I really must be off. Thank you again. Goodnight.'

'I'll see you out,' said James.

Claudia scrambled to her feet. 'I'll come with you.'

James shook his head. 'I need to finalise arrangements with Harriet.'

She sat down again abruptly, hiding her flush of mortification behind the fall of pale hair.

'Do come and see us again soon,' said Moira, as Harriet left.

'But you obviously don't want to come here again, do you?' demanded James as he saw Harriet to her car.

'No, I don't,' she said frankly. 'I like your sister and her husband very much, Lily too. Claudia obviously resents me due to this "fling" you mentioned, but the main reason is you, James. You still bear me a grudge.'

His face hardened in the bright security lights. 'Do you blame me?'

'Not in the least.' Harriet slid into the car, switched on the ignition and opened the window. 'Saturday then.'

'Saturday it is.' He gave her an unsettling smile. 'I'll be there on the stroke of ten. I'm really looking forward to meeting your father.'

His parting words sent chills down Harriet's spine as she drove home. Did he intend coming to River House on Saturday for a showdown with her father before cancelling the party? Harriet shivered at the prospect, though she knew exactly why James had asked her to the Old Rectory. He could easily have obtained the information he wanted during a phone call, but instead he had wanted, maybe needed, to demonstrate that he now had a family background like hers. And that he was the object of the sexy Claudia's passion. He needn't have bothered about the last. Harriet had no doubt that he'd been the object of several women's passion over the years. In his twenties he'd been attractive enough, but now he was ten years older he took her breath away.

CHAPTER THREE

ONCE informed of the new venture, Margaret Rogers, well aware of the difficult financial situation and most other things about the Wilde family, began on a frenzy of unnecessary cleaning. The furniture in every room was polished to an even higher gleam, and her husband was called in to wash the windows inside and out. The copper pans above the island in the kitchen were scoured to blinding glory, and Aubrey Wilde volunteered to eat out until after Saturday to keep the kitchen pristine. When Harriet got home on the Friday evening Margaret was waiting to take her on a tour of inspection. River House was looking its best from every possible point of view in the evening sunshine, the hall and drawing room fragrant with the arrangements made by Margaret from blooms and greenery Will had cut in the garden.

'How hard you've worked. It all looks wonderful,' said Harriet gratefully.

In Julia's bedroom they stood on the balcony outside the window and looked down on the gardens, which sloped down to the river which gave the house its name.

'Don't you miss living up here, Harriet?' Margaret asked. 'It still worries me to think of you alone down in that little place.'

'I like it there.'

'But surely you'll get married one day. You can't act as clerk of the works for the house for ever. It's not my place to say so, but it's not natural for a girl to carry such a load on her shoulders.'

'I promised I would,' said Harriet.

'I know.' The other woman nodded sadly. 'Your mother would want you to have a life, just the same.' She patted Harriet's hand. 'No offence.'

'Of course not,' said Harriet affectionately. 'Thank you for everything, Margaret. I don't know what my father would do without you.'

'I don't do it for him, dear; I made a promise, too.' Margaret smiled briskly. 'And now I must get home and prepare supper for John.'

'Please thank him for me. He's been a huge help.' And would be paid for it, no matter how much he protested.

Her father intercepted her on her way out. 'Since this telecoms chap wants a marquee, let's take a stroll round the garden.'

The herbaceous borders edging the lawns in front of the house were just coming into colour. Harriet breathed in the heady scent of newly cut grass as she tried to look at the gardens with the eye of a prospective client. 'John's done a great job with the weeding. Will says he wouldn't have managed it all in time without him.'

'Good man,' said Aubrey, and gave her a sidelong look. 'He'll need to be paid.'

'Of course. Now he's retired, he can do with the money.'

They went on to walk round the four acres of garden together, a new experience to them both recently. It was years since Harriet had spent any real time alone in her father's company. When they got back to the house he suggested a look round inside, but she told him she'd been over it earlier with Margaret.

'She's done even more wonders than usual, the house looks perfect.'

'But it's not,' said her father heavily. 'It would only be perfect if you came back home to live in it.'

She shook her head. 'Not going to happen. Goodnight. I'll see you in the morning.'

Next morning Harriet woke to the feeling of a cloud hanging over her and groaned at the thought of the morning ahead. In the shower she thought, not for the first time, that the only thing likely to drive her back to live in River House was the lure of a long hot soak in the kind of tub her bathroom was too small to accommodate. She dealt with her hair, tied it back in a skein of half damp curls, dressed in white shirt and jeans and ate some breakfast to get a kick-start to this important day. She couldn't rid herself of the feeling that James intended turning River House down once he'd inspected it. Thank God he still had no idea her father had once been ready to threaten him with arrest.

Harriet walked up to the house shortly before ten to find her father pacing along the terrace, smartly dressed as always, but visibly tense.

'Good morning.' He smiled warily. 'You look very young and pretty today.'

'Thank you. You look good yourself.' Her father never stinted on his wardrobe. 'Luckily the weather forecast was accurate for once. The gardens look fabulous in this sunshine. Will has worked incredibly hard.' She tensed at the sound of a car engine changing gears on the bend of the steep drive. 'Our client's arrived.'

Harriet waited with her father at the head of the steps, very much aware that his tension equalled her own. When James got out of a black convertible, wearing clothes much like hers, she saw her father relax and wished she could do the same.

'Looks like a decent sort of chap—that's an Aston Martin Volante,' he said in an undertone, and Harriet stood rigid with apprehension as James mounted the steps towards them. 'Good morning,' said her father, smiling genially. 'Welcome to River House. I'm Aubrey Wilde.'

'James Crawford.' James returned the smile, looking at him steadily as he shook hands. 'I've already met your daughter, of course. Good morning, Miss Wilde.'

She forced her stiff lips to smile. 'Good morning. Isn't it a lovely day? Shall we start the tour in the garden, or would you prefer to see over the house first?'

'The gardens, please. With luck, the weather will be good on the day and we'll have no need to trespass in the house.'

'We won't look on it as trespass, Crawford,' Aubrey assured him. 'Come in and look around. Harriet will give you the grand tour, and then we can have coffee before going on to the gardens.'

One look at James had been reassurance enough for her father. He was obviously still in blissful ignorance about James's identity, but it was equally obvious that he was now reconciled to letting out River House to him. 'Is that all right with you?' she asked James.

He smiled blandly. 'Of course. It would be a pleasure.'

'Splendid.' Aubrey led the way inside. 'Come back to the kitchen when you're ready and I'll have coffee waiting.'

'If you'll come this way, then, Mr Crawford,' said Harriet, and led him along the right-angled hall towards the drawing room at the far end.

'He hasn't a clue who he's dealing with, has he?' murmured James as they entered a vast sunlit room furnished with comfortable modern pieces living in harmony with the paintings and antiques handed down through Sarah Tolliver Wilde's family.

'Do you want me to tell him?'

'Not if it will make things difficult for you.' James took in the room, his smile bleak. 'Now I see inside this place at last, I understand why you couldn't give it up. But why the hell do you live in the Lodge now?'

'Personal reasons. Now, if you'll follow me back down the hall, the dining room is next on the left. Father insists on eating there every night when he's home.'

'Good God,' said James, following her into a large room with a table big enough for a board meeting. 'Do you eat here with him?'

'No.'

He looked down into her averted face. 'You've changed a lot, Harriet.'

'After all these years, that's hardly surprising.' She shrugged. 'You told me to grow up, so I did. Next along is Father's study—'

'We needn't go in there,' James said quickly.

'Follow me upstairs, then.'

He shook his head. 'It's unnecessary to see more of the house. Let's concentrate on the gardens.'

'As you wish.' She smiled brightly. 'Shall we have that coffee first?'

Aubrey Wilde was in a convivial mood when they entered the kitchen. 'I hope you don't mind drinking your coffee in here.'

James looked at the balloon chairs ranged around a mahogany table at one end, the oak cupboards and creamy counters lining the business end, and the island with gas hobs and canopy hung with gleaming copper pans. 'Only too pleased. Do you do much cooking, sir?'

Aubrey laughed, smiling sheepishly at his daughter.

'Afraid not. My wonderful Mrs Rogers does that—been with the family for years.'

Harriet supplied her father with the sweetened brew of his choice, then looked at James in polite question. 'How do you like yours?' Though she knew from their meeting that James took his coffee black, as he'd always done. And the look he gave her said he was well aware of it.

'As it comes, please.'

The two men chatted for a while, but after a few minutes James stood up. 'If you're ready for the tour now, Mr Wilde, I need to be off shortly.'

Aubrey sprang to attention. 'Of course, of course.'

Harriet got to her feet quickly, determined not leave them alone together. 'If you're keen to get away, Father, I'll take Mr Crawford over the gardens.'

'Splendid. You know more about them than me, anyway,' said her father. 'Don't forget the paddock.'

James thanked him formally and then followed Harriet down the steps to the main lawn to start the tour of the garden. She breathed a sigh of relief when she heard her father's car start up. It seemed certain, now, that James would keep to his decision to use River House for his party. And her father had no idea who he was, probably because he had simply erased her rebellion from his mind. Not impossible. Her father was an expert at airbrushing unpleasantness from his life.

It was a strange experience to show James round the extensive gardens he had never set foot in before. During their time together in the past she had been so determined to keep their relationship a secret she had always driven to meet him and never allowed him to take her home. His visit to the Lodge to mend her computer had been his sole time spent on the property.

'It's a lot bigger than I thought,' he commented as they crossed the vast lawn. 'A marquee will be no problem here.'

'No. My father could have given you more details about that, but—'

'But you wanted to get him away from me as soon as you could, in case he recognised me and cancelled the whole thing. Is it that important to you, Harriet?'

'Yes.' Her chin lifted proudly. 'We need a new roof.'

'And you're willing to take my money to pay for it.'

'Yes.' She led the way up the steps to the terrace, desperate now for him to leave so she could recover from the tension of the morning. As they reached the Lodge, Harriet looked up at him in query. 'Have you seen all you need to see?'

'Not exactly. May I come in?'

'Of course.' What else could she say? She opened the door and went ahead of him into her small sitting room.

'It looks very different in here now,' he commented, looking round.

'I've stamped my personality on it over the years.'

'Years?' James frowned. 'How long have you been living here?'

'I used it to study in as a teenager, if you remember, but since I qualified the Lodge has been my permanent home.'

'May I sit down?'

'Of course. Take the sofa.' Harriet curled up on the window seat.

'You had a desk in here,' he observed, after a silence a shade too long for comfort.

'It lives in my bedroom these days.' She eyed him warily. 'Is there anything else you need?'

'Yes, a chat.' James leaned back, irritatingly at ease as he dominated the room just by sitting there. 'When I introduced myself this morning I fully expected to be run off the property. It was an anticlimax to find your father obviously didn't know me from Adam.'

Harriet nodded. 'I only spoke about you once in the past, when I said I was going to live with you. I just referred to you as James.' She frowned. 'But he must have known your full name to get your boss to fire you—or transfer you, as it turned out.'

James shrugged. 'He just told George Lassiter to fire the techie who dared to have designs on his daughter. George knew exactly who came to River House that day, so maybe my surname never came into it.'

'You're probably right,' she agreed, and smiled. 'But I was wound a bit tight before you came.' For more reasons than he knew.

'I could tell.' James eyed her thoughtfully. 'If you won't live up in that wonderful house with your father, why the hell do you stay here, Harriet? It can't be filial loyalty, because even to the casual observer—which I'm not—it's obvious that the two of you aren't close.'

'I love the house.'

He raised an eyebrow. 'The house you refuse to live in. Are you hoping to inherit it one day?'

'I have two sisters,' she reminded him. 'The estate will be divided between us.' She slid to her feet. 'Would you like a drink?'

'No, thanks. I'd better be on my way.' He stood up, crowding her enough to make Harriet claustrophobic. 'It's been good to see you again.'

'Has it? I thought you still harboured old resentments,' she said lightly.

James shook his head. 'Not any more. You were only a kid when we broke up, and now I've been over River House I understand why you couldn't leave it.'

'Actually, you don't,' she informed him, and moved to the door.

He stood in her way. 'Enlighten me, then.'

'There's no point. It was all a long time ago.' She smiled brightly. 'You've come a very long way since then, while I'm still here where we first met.'

'And I still want to know why.' For the first time since meeting her again he gave her the smile which had once made her fall so helplessly in love with him.

Harriet shook her head. 'It's no big mystery, but still not one I intend to share.' With anyone, least of all with a forceful, successful man like James Crawford. The truth was simple. Her father revelled in the cachet of a home like River House, but not in the responsibility of looking after it. She held the door wider as James moved to stand beside her.

She flinched as he took a strand of her hair and pulled it out straight before letting it spring back into a curl. 'I always liked doing that. Your hair is the only thing about you that hasn't changed.'

'Hardly surprising. I was a teenager when we knew each other, James. Now I'm an adult and an accountant. Not a profession known for glamour—as Claudia pointed out.'

He grinned. 'She got to you, did she?' His smiled faded as she deliberately backed to put space between them.

'Before you go, James, tell me the truth. Why did you hire River House?'

He shrugged. 'I'm a businessman, Harriet. I met Charlotte Brewster, got interested in what she does for a living, and told her what I had in mind for a party. She suggested your place as the ideal location, and for obvious reasons I jumped at the chance.' He eyed her challengingly. 'I'll have invitations sent to you and your father. Will you come, or will you hide away while the party's on?'

Secretly euphoric that he had no intention of cancelling, she smiled brightly. 'Thank you for the invitation—I'd love to come.'

James drove off deep in thought. His motive in hiring River House had been simple. It had been a heaven-sent opportunity to pay the Wildes back for their treatment of him all those years ago. His original intention, once the party was over, had been to make sure Aubrey Wilde knew exactly who'd paid him good money to hire his house, and then get the hell out of the place and never look back. But meeting up with Harriet again had changed all that. All buttoned up in her accountant persona she'd affected him enough, but the moment he'd seen her today in shirt and jeans, hair loose and looking like the girl he'd once adored, his mind was made up. With Moira living so close to hand it would be easy to come and go on Harriet's territory and see what developed.

CHAPTER FOUR

NICK CORBETT was relatively new to the town. Since the day he had taken over from Aubrey Wilde at the bank, he'd also adopted a proprietorial attitude towards Harriet, who found it rather amusing, and made no objection to spending the occasional evening in his company. His fair hair and bright blue eyes gave him a deceptive look of youth which, coupled with his easy manner and single status, had soon made him a great favourite socially. Harriet saw that tonight, as usual, she was the object of more than one envious look as he ushered her into the bar of the King's Head.

'This is good,' he said, after the waiter brought their drinks. 'I always feel so relaxed in your company, Harriet. Which I suppose isn't surprising. I inherited your father's job, so you could say I'm almost part of the family.'

'A bit of a stretch,' said Harriet, laughing.

'You look amazingly different with your hair like that,' he said, leaning closer. 'You should let it loose more often.'

She shrugged. 'Wouldn't jibe with my accountant persona.'

He laughed, and moved closer to study the menu with her. 'What do you fancy tonight?'

'Practically anything—other than organs!'

His crack of laughter brought heads swivelling in their direction. 'I'm with you there! And don't look now, but there's some chap at the bar looking our way. Friend of yours?'

Harriet's spirits plummeted when she saw James at the bar with Claudia. He nodded coolly as their eyes met and slid an arm round his companion's waist to lead her away.

'You know him?' asked Nick.

'He's an acquaintance, yes.'

The arrival of a waiter distracted Nick from any further speculation until they were in the dining room, where the entire Graveney family was dining with James. Lily alerted Moira and Marcus, who both waved, smiling. Harriet waved back, and Claudia moved closer to James, her smile a mere flash of teeth.

'Just an acquaintance?' murmured Nick.

'Actually he's a sort of client,' said Harriet, resigned, and explained the connection. The takeover of River House for a party would soon be breaking news in the town anyway.

'So *he's* James Crawford,' said Nick, impressed. 'I've read quite a bit about him recently—quite a success story. But why is he using your house for his party?'

'A client of mine suggested it to him as a venue with a difference.'

'And your father actually agreed to it?'

'Only after much persuasion.' Harriet smiled brightly. 'Here comes our dinner.'

For the third time that week Harriet failed to enjoy a meal she would normally have eaten with pleasure. It was James's fault, she thought morosely, and summoned a bright smile when the Graveneys stopped at the table with James on their way out. Harriet looked on in amusement as Nick flirted with Claudia and Lily, shook hands with the Graveneys, and finally, inevitably, with James Crawford, who spoke to Nick for a moment before turning to Harriet.

'I'm leaving tomorrow, Miss Wilde. I'll be back in good

time for the big day. You have my numbers, so don't hesitate to call if you have questions.'

'Of course.' Harriet gave him her bland professional smile, but infused more warmth as she turned to Moira. 'Will you be at the party?'

'Wouldn't miss it for the world, Harriet.'

'We'll all be there,' interrupted Claudia with a triumphant smile.

'Wild horses couldn't keep *you* away!' scoffed Lily.

'Come on, girls,' said their brother. 'Good to see you again, Harriet.'

'Please come to see us again soon,' said Moira warmly.

'You're very kind, I'll take you up on that one day,' Harriet promised, avoiding James's cynical eye.

Alone again, Nick regarded Harriet with interest. 'How long have you actually known Crawford?'

'I met him briefly years ago, when I was a student.'

'The hot blonde with him was pretty cold towards you!'

'Was she? I didn't notice.' Harriet stood up swiftly. 'Thanks for the meal, Nick. If you'll walk me out to the car I'll be on my way.'

He sprang to his feet, crestfallen. 'It's early yet, Harriet. I hoped you'd come back to my place for coffee.'

'Not tonight.' Harriet smiled up at him as he saw her to the door. 'Thanks again.'

'Let's do this again soon.'

'Of course. Ring me. Goodnight.'

Harriet drove home in thoughtful mood. Running into James again tonight had put a definite damper on her evening, and Nick had been very much aware of it. Not that she would have gone back to his place even if she hadn't seen James. Nick had been in an odd mood from the moment he'd seen her tonight. It had been a bad idea to wear her hair loose. She sighed as she turned into the carport alongside the Lodge. She'd be tempted to have it cut if she didn't know exactly what would happen. She'd tried that at her lowest ebb after the break up with James, and the result had been a halo of unruly curls which would look even more ludicrous now that she was ten years older.

As the date of the party grew nearer Harriet was surprised to find that her father was relishing the idea, rather than objecting to it. And when Charlotte Brewster came up with a list of further money-making possibilities he was actually delighted with the idea of a television cookery programme taking place in his own kitchen.

'Hard to believe,' said Harriet, reporting to Julia, 'but he's all for it.'

'And are you happy about people using Mother's beloved kitchen?'

'Why not? She'd be delighted if it shored up our finances.'

'You're right. By the way, what's Miriam's take on the new venture?' Julia asked.

'She's not back from her cruise yet.'

Julia laughed. 'I bet there'll be hell to pay when she is. By the way, if you're going to this party, what are you wearing?'

'The dress I wore when you saw me last.'

'It's not a party dress, Harriet. For heaven's sake buy something new.'

'Can't stretch to it right now.'

There was a pause. 'I assume extra wages were necessary to get the house and garden in trim. Have they come out of your own pocket?'

Harriet sighed. 'Guilty as charged, Julia. I need this event to be a success to advertise our wares to other customers. And a house and garden in perfect shape was part of the deal.'

'Have you organised press coverage?'

'Charlotte saw to that.'

In addition to the local press, a reporter from one of the nationals would be on hand on the day, information which gave such pleasure to Aubrey Wilde it was hard to remember his original opposition to the project.

Later that evening James rang to say that the marquee people would be turning up first thing in the morning.

'Fine. I won't be here, but I'll tell Father. Are you coming with them?'

'No. I'm tied up tomorrow, but my assistant will oversee things. How's the garden looking? I gather you've had some rain in the locality lately.'

'Just enough to perk up the flowers and green the grass a bit. Will Haines cut it again for me yesterday,' she said.

'Who's he?'

'Gardener. He comes one day a week.'

'Just *one* day?' he exclaimed.

'He's been doing extra lately.'

'He must have done a hell of a lot extra to get the place looking so good.' James paused. 'Your father's not into gardening, I take it.'

'No. He prefers golf.' It was Harriet who rode the sit-on lawnmower at weekends to free Will for other work.

There was silence for a moment. 'Don't change your mind about turning up on Saturday.'

Or what? 'I said I'll be there,' she said tartly, 'if only to make sure nothing goes wrong.'

'I'll have security people there for that, so you can just relax and enjoy the evening. By the way, shall I send an invitation to the little friend you were dining with last week? I'm afraid I've forgotten his name.'

Harriet rolled her eyes. 'That won't be necessary. Was there anything else?'

'Not at the moment. I'll be in touch.'

Harriet disconnected and shook her head in wonder. How strange that it was now possible to hold a perfectly ordinary conversation with the man she'd been so madly in love with all those years ago. Though his remark about Nick Corbett had been a pejorative. It was Nick's misfortune that James Crawford put him in the shade by sheer force of personality as well as size. But at least Nick was unattached, which James was not, if Claudia's behaviour was anything to go by. Harriet sighed, wishing now she hadn't promised her father to put in an appearance on Saturday. Maybe she could dash out in her lunch hour tomorrow and buy a dress. She shook her head firmly. No. She would not spend money on something so unnecessary. It was hardly the school prom. And no one would care what she wore, anyway.

The following morning Margaret rang Harriet at the office, an event so rare Harriet went cold, fearing the worst.

'What's wrong, Margaret?'

'Nothing at all, dear. I'm just letting you know that a courier brought a parcel up here to the house when he couldn't get an answer at the Lodge. He needed a signature. Shall I tell John to run it down to you at the office?'

'No need to bother him. I haven't ordered anything, so it isn't urgent. Could you just pop it down to the Lodge on your way home?'

'Of course. The marquee firm is here, by the way. Your father's down on the main lawn, directing operations.'

'He'll enjoy that.'

'I hope all goes well tomorrow, Harriet.'

'Me too, Margaret. I can't tell you how grateful I am for all the work you and John have put in over this.'

'We were glad to do it. You just enjoy the party,' the other woman urged.

Harriet very much doubted that she would. Watching James host a party at River House was daunting on several different levels. His motive for inviting her was plain enough. He wanted Harriet Wilde and her father to witness his success in the one location guaranteed to make the celebration doubly triumphant for him. But she couldn't rid herself of the worry that he intended to use the occasion to humiliate the Wildes in some way. Harriet deliberately worked late that evening to make sure her father would be out when she got home, in case he felt the need to show her the marquee. But when she turned up the drive to the Lodge at last it was James who was waiting to do that.

'Come and make sure everything is to your satisfaction now the marquee is up,' he said as she got out of her car.

'Shouldn't that be to your satisfaction?' she said wryly. 'It's your party, and your money—'

'But your house.' He looked at his watch. 'You're very late, Harriet.'

'I had things to clear up before I left the office,' she lied.

James eyed her sternly. 'You look tired.'

Harriet glared. 'I wish you wouldn't keep saying that. Of course I'm tired. I work hard. And I'm ten years older than I was back then.'

'When you let your hair down you don't look it—' He stopped, eyes narrowed. 'What have I said to put that look on your face?'

'There's more to me than just hair,' she snapped. 'Now, let's inspect this marquee so I can get on with my evening.'

'I wouldn't dream of keeping you,' he said coldly. 'Inspect it yourself in the morning. Goodnight.' He strode off to the marquee, wondering why he couldn't get the damn woman out of his mind now he'd met up with her again. He had been so sure that if they met up again she would mean nothing more to him than a mistake he'd made in the past. But one look at her in the bank that day had turned the clock back to the time when he'd wanted nothing more in life than to share it with Harriet Wilde. And now he found himself seeking opportunities to see her again, just like the lovesick idiot he had once been. Once the party was over that would definitely have to stop.

Cursing herself for losing her temper, Harriet let herself into the Lodge as James strode off, dumped down her briefcase and with a sigh pulled the pins out of her hair and ran her fingers through it as she always did the moment she was through the door. A tempting little savoury tart was waiting in the kitchen, courtesy of Margaret, a thoughtful touch which brought tears to Harriet's eyes as she made coffee. She was more tired than she thought. But when she took her mug into the other room the tears dried like magic. The mysterious parcel was waiting on the sofa.

Suddenly as excited as a child, Harriet put the mug down and carefully slit open the parcel wrapping to reveal a very smart box with a note from Julia tucked into the swathes of tissue paper inside:

You may think of me as one of the Ugly Sisters, Cinderella, but just this once I'm Fairy Godmother. Enclosed a sample frock I got hold of, regretfully too small for me. Buy frivolous shoes, wear that hair down and have a ball!

Harriet took out the dress and laid it reverently over the back of the sofa. It was a slip of a dress, scoop necked and sleeveless in tawny red pure silk satin. She ran up the short flight of stairs to her bedroom, stripped off her clothes and stepped into the dress. It skimmed her knees and fitted so exactly it could have been made for her. She stared, delighted, at her reflection, and then rang Julia.

'You just caught me, Harriet. I'm on my way out. You received the parcel?'

'I certainly did; it was a marvellous surprise. Thanks a lot. Is the dress very expensive?'

'Not to you, Cinderella. Regard it as an early birthday present. Does it fit?'

'Perfectly.'

'Then look on it as my contribution to the general cause. Fly the Wilde flag with pride tomorrow and have fun.'

This was a bigger ask than Julia knew. 'I will. Thanks again. I owe you.'

Harriet removed the dress with great care, then got into jeans and a sweater to toss some salad to eat with her tart. Before she could make a start on it, the doorbell rang. With a sigh she opened the door to her godmother, who pushed past her, bristling with indignation.

'What on earth is going on, Harriet? Why is there a marquee?' demanded Miriam Cairns indignantly. 'If Aubrey is throwing a party why haven't I been invited?'

'It's not Father's party, Miriam. Did you enjoy your cruise? When did you get back? Can I make you a sandwich or something? I was just about to eat my supper.'

'I got back yesterday. Nothing to eat, thanks, but a drink would be lovely. Do you have any decent sherry?'

'Sorry, not even indecent sherry. Tea instead?'

Miriam sat down on the sofa, her handsome features troubled. 'Tea's fine. Then eat your supper; you look tired.'

Harriet scowled as she switched on the kettle. She was *really* tired of people telling her she looked tired. In no mood to bother with a teapot and get out the china cups

Miriam would have preferred, she made tea in a mug and took it in to her godmother.

'Thank you, dear. Now for heaven's sake tell me what's going on.'

Harriet carried her supper over to the window seat and ate while she explained. For once Miriam actually heard her out to the end without interruption, bar the odd exclamation.

'Well, well,' she said at last, eyes narrowed. 'So Aubrey's been forced to toe the line at last! I knew he'd lost heavily over some shares, but I had no idea he'd run through everything Sarah left him. Why haven't you told me about this before? If nothing else, I could have lent a sympathetic ear.' Miriam eyed her goddaughter militantly. 'Sarah told me everything, always. She would want you to confide in me.'

Harriet gazed back, unmoved. 'I tried that in the past, if you remember, and got short shrift.'

'Good God, are you still harping on about that, child? It was years ago. If you'd been allowed to go your own way then by now you'd be living in some dreary little house cooking meals for your husband and children, with never a penny to spare...' Miriam came to a sudden halt.

'Instead, I live alone in this little house, with no children, no husband, I work hard to support myself and there's still no penny to spare,' said Harriet flatly. 'We're in urgent need of money to repair the roof, Miriam, so I resorted to shock tactics to persuade Father to let someone pay through the nose to hire the house for this party. And if it's a success and attracts publicity, hopefully more people will pay to do the same.'

'And all because you promised Sarah you'd take care of her family home.' Miriam's mouth set. 'She knew you were the only one who would.' She sniffed. 'Aubrey was just a bank clerk when she met him—terribly handsome then, of course. And Sarah was not only pretty, she was Miss Tolliver of River House. Aubrey Wilde, as you well know, came from a humbler background and wanted bigger things. Sarah was the key to a whole new lifestyle for him, and he made sure he got her.'

This was new. 'What do you mean?'

'Oh, come on, dear. Why do you think her father let Sarah marry a nobody like Aubrey?' Miriam nodded maliciously as comprehension dawned in Harriet's eyes. 'When Sarah told her father she was pregnant he had no choice. He pulled strings to get promotion for Aubrey, but he was never reconciled to the match. Aubrey did his best to fit in—imitated Sarah's speech patterns and even adopted her father's style of dressing, but Godfrey Tolliver remained unimpressed. Not that Aubrey cared a damn once he had his foot in the door at River House.' She gave a mirthless little laugh. 'Perhaps you can see now why he went berserk when you announced you were taking off with some lad who repaired computers—history repeating itself!'

Harriet eyed her coolly. 'You weren't keen on the idea either.'

'True. I sincerely thought it was best to wait—'

'Unfortunately, my man wouldn't do that.'

'Which only shows you were well rid of him.' Miriam put her mug down on the small table beside her. 'Have you ever met up with him again?'

Harriet nodded. 'Quite recently.'

Miriam rolled her eyes. 'So who is he? Honestly, girl, it's like getting blood out of a stone. I never did find out who he was. You were very clever at keeping your mystery boyfriend out of the way.'

'Because I knew exactly what would happen if you and

Father got involved.' Harriet's dark Tolliver eyes flashed. 'And it did.'

'But you're over all that now, surely!'

'Oh, definitely. He's right out of my league these days.' Harriet smiled sweetly. 'He's now the head of the Live Wires Group, the one paying Father good money to hire River House for a party tomorrow.'

'Good God, are you *serious*?' Miriam stared, thunderstruck. 'Aubrey actually agreed to this?'

'Yes.'

'Has he met the man?'

'Yes. James came here to consult with him about the party, announced his name and shook my father's hand. But I'd taken good care that Father never knew his name back then. As far as he's concerned, James Crawford is just the man paying lovely money for the privilege of hiring the Wilde family home. Father's even accepted an invitation to the party tomorrow night.'

Miriam shook her head in wonder. 'When are you going to tell him?'

'I'm not planning to tell him. He'll find out in due course. Not that it will matter if—when—he does. He signed a contract, and most of the money has already been paid into a separate business account only I can draw on for the upkeep of River House,' Harriet said with satisfaction. 'Julia is in full support on this.'

'That's new. You girls have never been close.'

'Julia, at least, had a change of heart when she discovered the situation was so desperate. She even sent me a dress to wear tomorrow night.'

'In her line of business it probably didn't cost her anything,' Miriam muttered.

'But she thought of it, and it didn't cost me anything, either.'

Miriam got up. 'I've got a good mind to go up to Aubrey right now and ask him what he meant by letting things get so much out of hand—'

'He's out and won't be home until late,' said Harriet hastily.

'As usual! I'll be off, then, and let you get to bed. Sleep late for once in the morning so you look your best tomorrow night. Though I'm surprised you agreed to go.'

'I need to keep an eye on things.'

'Or are you still hankering after this man?' Miriam asked shrewdly.

'As it happens, I'm not.' Harriet smiled sweetly. 'But, even if I were, it would be my choice to do so, Godmother. I'm not nineteen any more.'

Miriam shook her head sadly. 'You're an unforgiving soul.'

'As Father has long since discovered.'

CHAPTER FIVE

HARRIET'S plan to get up late next morning was foiled by traffic passing under her bedroom window with deliveries for the party. At last she gave up and got dressed, read the morning paper over breakfast, walked up to the terrace to watch operations afterwards, and found her father doing the same thing.

'Good morning, Harriet.'

'Good morning. I thought you might have been down there on the lawn directing operations.'

'I did that when they installed the marquee. I shan't put my nose in with the catering people. It's a formal dinner, thank God.'

Harriet's eyebrows rose. 'What else did you expect?'

'A chap at the club told me that on top of his daughter's wedding breakfast he had to provide a fish and chip van and a burger bar later on for the younger set.' Aubrey grimaced. 'But Crawford seems too civilised for that kind of thing.'

They watched the activity down below as the caterers set up their mobile kitchen, and the 'facilities' James had mentioned were discreetly stationed behind the row of trees on the far side of the lawn. Harriet tensed as a familiar car came up the drive to park near them, and James got out, followed by Lily, who came running towards Harriet, smiling eagerly.

'I hope you don't mind. When James said he was coming to check we made him bring us too. Good morning, I'm Lily Graveney,' she added, holding out her hand to Aubrey. 'You're obviously Mr Wilde, Harriet's father. How do you do?'

Aubrey gave her his best smile as he took her hand. 'Delighted to meet you. And who is this lovely young lady?' he added as Claudia joined them.

'I'm Lily's sister,' she informed him.

'Welcome to you both, and to you, Crawford,' Aubrey added, as James joined them.

'Thank you, sir. Sorry to intrude this early, but I had to make sure all was going smoothly, and these two insisted on coming with me.' James turned to Harriet. 'Good morning. I hope you weren't disturbed too early.'

'Not a problem,' said Aubrey jovially. 'Harriet's always up with the lark anyway.'

'Even on Saturdays?' said Claudia.

Harriet shook her head. 'No. Normally I enjoy a more leisurely start at the weekend.'

'But I've put paid to that today,' said James, frowning.

'She can have a nap this afternoon,' said Aubrey airily. 'Now, if you'll forgive me, I must get off—due at the club shortly.'

'We'll see you tonight, sir,' said James, and turned to Harriet. 'Would you care to take a look in the marquee with us?'

'I'll wait to see it lit up in all its glory tonight.'

James nodded coolly. 'As you wish. Come, girls.'

Claudia thrust a possessive hand through his arm, but Lily loitered behind to look up at the house. 'You have such a beautiful home, Harriet. See you later.'

* * *

Harriet went indoors and locked River House securely behind her, suddenly in the mood to spend the day down in
the town while the unsettling bustle was going on. But if
the new venture was a success this kind of disruption would
be part of life at River House from now on. She shrugged.
As long as the disruption brought in money for repairs and
maintenance she would live with it. Happily.

Harriet got home later that afternoon to the sound of
piano music in the marquee. She strolled up the drive to
the terrace, which now held a bar at one end, ready for the
influx of guests later. Lights had been strung in the trees
below, and there was an infectious expectancy in the air.
She breathed it in and smiled. If she had to be at the party
tonight she might as well enjoy it. As she turned to walk
back her father came hurrying out of the house.

'I'm glad I spotted you, Harriet. Should I wear black tie
tonight?'

She shook her head. 'This is a party for James Crawford's
workforce, Father. I imagine it will be less formal than that.
Just wear one of your suits.' Lord knew, any one of them
was expensive and elegant enough for the occasion.

'You're right,' he said, nodding. 'Are you wearing an
evening gown?'

'No, Father. Don't worry. I won't let you down.'

His mouth tightened. 'I never imagined you would.'

'By the way, Miriam came to see me last night,' Harriet
informed him. 'She was furious when she saw the marquee—thought you were having a party and hadn't invited
her.'

Aubrey snorted. 'As though I'd dare! What did she say
when you explained?'

'Quite a lot. You know Miriam.'

'I do indeed.'

'I'd better get back and think about getting ready. You

had a very short game today,' Harriet added, surprised when he flushed slightly.

'I wasn't actually playing; just having lunch with a friend.'

Harriet's eyebrows rose as she walked down to the Lodge. Her father often had lunch at the club with a friend. Why so shifty?

Harriet was almost ready later when she heard piano music vying with the chatter and laughter of the guests as they were conducted from the paddock car park. She zipped up the dress, fastened on her mother's pearl and diamond earrings and slid her feet into the nude heels bought earlier from the shop that sold ruinously expensive footwear in the arcade near the market hall. Pleased to see they made her legs look yards long, she went downstairs to open the door to her father, who looked resplendent in one of the dark suits he favoured. His eyes grew embarrassingly moist at the sight of her.

'You look so like your mother tonight, Harriet. You're a picture in that dress.'

'Julia sent it to me as a birthday present.'

Aubrey frowned. 'Good of her, but it's not your birthday yet.'

'No, Father, not for months.'

'I see.' Though he obviously didn't. 'Come, then; let's join the party. I suggest we go back through the house, and make an entrance via the front door.'

To show everyone who actually owned the house. Fair enough—it would be good PR. 'The last time we had champagne on the terrace was at Sophie's wedding,' Harriet remarked.

Her father stopped short halfway along the hall. 'Does Sophie know what's happening tonight?'

'No idea. Julia is keeping her up to date with events.'

'If she knew there was a party she would already be here,' said Aubrey wryly. He opened the front door and held it back for Harriet to go outside, but she stopped dead, blinded by a barrage of flash photography.

'Good heavens,' she muttered as they went down the path to the front steps. 'I didn't expect that.'

'I said you looked a picture,' said her father with unusual dryness.

There was more photography as James came to greet them with a look for Harriet which set her heart thumping under the glowing satin. 'You look wonderful, Miss Wilde. Good evening, sir. Come and meet my sister and her family.'

The Graveneys were drinking champagne with the girls, plus a young man who was holding Lily's hand.

'Mr Wilde, meet my sister Moira Graveney, and her husband Marcus,' said James. 'You've met Marcus's stepsisters already, and this is Dominic Hall, Lily's boyfriend.'

Moira, tall and elegant in dark blue silk, congratulated Aubrey Wilde on his beautiful home. 'It was kind of you to let James use it for his party.'

'Not at all, dear lady. Only too happy,' he assured her as he took her hand.

Marcus shook Harriet's hand, his eyes gleaming in appreciation. 'May I say you look ravishing tonight?'

'Indeed you may.' She smiled at him radiantly and turned to his sisters. 'So do you two.'

Lily laughed, fluffing out the skirt of her pink chiffon dress. 'You put us in the shade, Harriet.'

Claudia shrugged. 'We played safe.'

Safe? In impossibly high heels and a black strapless dress with an outrageously short skirt, Claudia Graveney looked downright dangerous to Harriet.

James made sure they were supplied with drinks, and then excused himself to mingle with his employees. Harriet watched him over her glass as he stopped here and there, chatting with people who obviously felt at ease in his company.

Moira moved close. 'On these occasions James always takes care to make sure everyone's enjoying themselves.'

'Does he throw parties often?'

'Usually just twice a year. This is a one-off.'

In more ways than one, thought Harriet, and felt a shiver of apprehension as she watching the tall figure she had never thought to meet again in any circumstances, let alone in a party he was hosting at her own home. 'Who is the young man circulating with your brother?'

'His personal assistant, David Walker.' Moira refused as she was offered more champagne. 'How about you, Harriet?'

'Just between you and me, I don't really care for it. I'll just nurse my glass.'

'I'll do the same,' confessed Moira. 'At my own wedding earlier this year I kept to lemonade.'

'Are you discussing your drinking habits, wife?' said her husband.

'I sympathise with Moira,' said Harriet, smiling at him. 'I'm very popular when I go out with friends. I drive them home afterwards.'

'It's difficult to avoid alcohol at certain times,' said Moira ruefully. 'At my brother's wedding I drank the toast rather than make a fuss.'

Harriet suddenly felt as if she were in a lift hurtling down to ground level. 'One has to sometimes,' she agreed brightly, and downed the rest of her wine. James was *married*? Couldn't he have at least mentioned it—but then, why should he? It was nothing to do with her. Though why wasn't the woman here tonight? And why the devil was James messing about with Claudia? Harriet shot a look at the girl who was laughing for once with Lily and her boy-friend as she played up to admiring glances coming her way from several of the younger male guests. 'Where is his wife now?' she asked casually, and won a strange glance from both Graveneys.

'In Australia, dear. They're based in Sydney for a couple of years,' said Moira. 'The baby's too young to travel, so I haven't met him yet, alas.'

'You will soon,' said Marcus, smiling at Harriet. 'I've promised my wife a trip to Australia in place of the hon-eymoon we didn't have time to take earlier on. Once I'm fully established in Broad Street I'll start sorting out holi-day arrangements.'

'Dan says the baby's the image of him, but Kate swears he looks just like her,' said Moira, and took a photograph from her beaded clutch. 'I know it's boring to pass round baby snaps, but he's so sweet.'

Harriet's fingers shook as she took the photograph, which showed two proud parents smiling over the bundle held in his mother's arms. Dan, she thought, dazed. James's brother. 'How absolutely lovely,' she said with fervour as David Walker came up the steps to the terrace to announce that dinner was served. Aubrey Wilde held out his arm to Moira.

'Shall we, Mrs Graveney?'

'Moira, please,' she said, smiling. James came back to accompany his party down to the lawn and into the green-ery-lined walkway towards the sound of soft piano music coming from the marquee, which looked magical with flower-filled tables, glittering chandeliers and a galaxy of twinkling stars in the midnight blue ceiling.

'Wait here for a moment, please,' said David. 'I'll go in first and announce you.'

'Hell, no,' said James. 'We'll follow on like everyone else.'

'Right.' But David still managed to get a signal to the pianist. The moment James appeared there was a dramatic arpeggio down the keys to announce his arrival and everyone began applauding.

'Your brother's a popular man,' said Aubrey, impressed.

Moira nodded in misty-eyed agreement, and Harriet felt a pang of jealousy as sharp as a physical pain as Claudia gazed up at James with avid possession in her heavily painted eyes. She had to remember that he was nothing to do with her any more, married or not. She was shown to a chair between James and Marcus at the table of honour with Moira between her brother and Aubrey Wilde, and a pouting Claudia placed opposite, next to a young man James introduced to everyone as Tom Bradfield, his young development wizard. The girl would be obliged to talk to him, noted Harriet, hoping she would have the grace to do so. Dominic Hall on her other side was too absorbed in Lily to pay attention to her sister.

'Pray silence for Mr James Crawford,' David Walker announced, and Harriet tensed as James got to his feet to a barrage of flash photography. Her heart beat a frantic tattoo under the satin as she wondered if this was the moment he'd chosen to enlighten her father as to who, exactly, had paid to take over his home for the night. Instead, James took the opportunity to congratulate his original employees on their hard work, and at the same time welcome the new additions to the Live Wires Group workforce in celebration of a merger which would lead to even better and bigger things for the company in the future. Finally, with a bow to Harriet and her father, he raised his glass to toast

Mr Aubrey Wilde and Miss Harriet Wilde for allowing him to use their beautiful home to make the occasion doubly special.

James resumed his seat to tumultuous applause and, limp with relief, her fears set at rest, at least for now, and with Claudia half hidden by the flower centrepiece, Harriet felt she might actually enjoy the meal. With the piano music a muted background she chatted easily for a while to Marcus Graveney about his settling-in process in Broad Street, and then turned to James when he asked if she approved of the marquee.

'I certainly do. Thank heavens my sister isn't here. It's far grander than the one Father hired for Sophie's wedding.' She gave him a straight look. 'So, James. Are you happy now? Does all this give you the necessary satisfaction?'

'Not yet,' he muttered. 'Your father still has no idea who I am.'

'But *I* know. That's some satisfaction, surely?' Harriet gave him a bright smile, then turned to Marcus again.

When the meal was over there was a general rush outside before the rest of the evening began. Harriet took Moira and the girls up to the bathrooms in the house, and in response to Lily's eager request took them over the rest of it afterwards while the men enjoyed a cigar in the garden. When they returned to the marquee a small band was in position, ready to play for the rest of the evening.

'Do you like dancing, Harriet?' Marcus asked, eyes twinkling.

'When the occasion arises, yes,' she assured him, surprised when the band struck up a waltz. She swallowed a chuckle at the horror on Claudia's face.

'I'm catering for all age groups tonight,' said James blandly, and pushed back his chair. 'May I have the pleasure, Miss Wilde?'

Secretly as horrified as Claudia, Harriet smiled at the others in desperate appeal. 'Please join us.'

The dance floor was big for a marquee, but small to Harriet as James took her in his arms to revolve with skill she hadn't expected. Her heart resumed its tattoo again as he held her close. 'Where did you learn to waltz?' she muttered, shaken to the core just to be in his arms again.

'A kind lady in Newcastle taught me. She taught me other things, too, the kind not permitted on a dance floor,' he added in an undertone, his hand so warm on her back Harriet was afraid the satin would burn. 'After we broke up, I needed consolation. She provided it. How about you?'

'I learned in school.'

'I meant consolation. Or maybe you didn't need any.'

She looked up at him squarely. 'Of course I did, but I had no one to console me.'

He pulled her closer. 'Why are you trembling, Harriet?'

'Nerves at being the centre of attention,' she lied, grateful when more people took to the floor.

'You look ravishing tonight,' he said, which made the trembling worse.

'More like the girl you left behind?' she said lightly.

'No. She was a girl, Harriet, with no ravishing allowed, remember?' His eyes bored down into hers. 'Things are different now you're all woman.'

Harriet stared, mesmerised, into his narrowed, glittering eyes as they moved together, oblivious of everything other than the sensuous contact as they moved together. She came back to earth with a start as the rhythm changed, and James cursed under his breath.

'Hell. Whatever this is, my lessons never covered it.'

'It's a foxtrot.'

'We could jig about to it like the younger set, or would you like to sit down?'

'Sit, please,' she said, so fervently James gave her a wry, knowing look as he led her back to the now empty table.

'Was dancing with me such an ordeal, Harriet?'

'Of course not,' she lied serenely. The ordeal had been hiding her response to the heat of his body against hers.

'Your father's still in the dark about me, obviously. Will you tell him?'

'Not unless you want me to. He's bound to hear from someone sooner or later. He can kill some other messenger.'

He frowned darkly. 'Is he likely to turn violent if you tell him?'

She shook her head. 'I was speaking metaphorically. He's never raised a hand to me in his life. But it was so hard to persuade him to agree to this tonight I didn't risk enlightening him beforehand.'

'Why was his agreement so vital?'

'We need the money,' she said baldly, and shook her head as James offered a fresh bottle of champagne. 'No, thanks. I'd rather have some iced water from that jug.'

James eyed her closely as he filled a glass for her. 'Back then I assumed your family was very wealthy.'

'Comfortable rather than wealthy, but not even that any more. The recent financial situation played havoc with my father's investments.' She gave him a rueful smile. 'This party tonight may have satisfied your need to get your own back on the Wildes, but it provided me with money to pay for the roof, and hopefully it will attract other punters to hire River House so I can get more maintenance done.'

He frowned. 'It provided *you* with money, not your father?'

She nodded. 'The others are coming back, by the way, and Claudia's giving me the evil eye again. You'd better dance with her next.'

'In that dress? Not a chance. There was a major incident earlier when Marcus first laid eyes on it. She refused to change, so it's thanks to Moira that she's here at all.'

'Tricky. How does your sister cope with family crises?'

'Brilliantly. But then she's known the girls since they were babies. She was Marcus's personal assistant for years, long before she became his wife. His stepsisters are fond of her, thankfully, and their mother is, too. Louise has never been a wicked stepmother where Marcus is concerned.'

Harriet smiled at the others as they returned to the table, and then got to her feet with a smile when David Walker asked her to dance. He led her back on the floor to partner him in a lively quickstep, which eventually changed to a tango.

'I was in Argentina earlier this year and got hooked on this,' he informed her. 'Are you up for it, Miss Wilde?'

She was about to say no, then nodded, abruptly tired of her role as the quiet one in the family. 'Oddly enough, I am. When I was a student I joined a dance club and liked Latin American best. I hope I remember how—but go easy with the kicking bits, please.'

Dancing the tango, Harriet found, was only similar to riding a bike in that she hadn't forgotten how to do it. David was surprisingly skilful, she was wearing the perfect dress for it and, to her amusement, they drew glances of admiration from all the onlookers, bar two. James watched them with all the animation of a graven image, and Claudia, predictably, had a face like thunder. But when the other dancers cleared the floor to watch Harriet called a halt.

'I draw the line at providing the cabaret,' she said breathlessly, and David thanked her very warmly and led her back to the table.

'That was *wonderful*,' exclaimed Moira, and Harriet grinned as Marcus held her chair out for her.

'I haven't tangoed since I was a student. Good fun, though.'

'I had no idea you could dance like that,' said Aubrey Wilde, eyeing his daughter with awe.

'I joined a dance club in college. Even accountants need light relief sometimes!'

Lily looked delighted. 'They're playing a samba now, Harriet. Can you do that, too?'

'I can, but I'm not going to.'

'I can samba,' said Claudia promptly, jumping up. 'Come on, James. Dance with me.'

He shook his head. 'Not a chance. I only waltz.'

Tom leapt to his feet. 'Dance with me instead, Claudia?'

For a horrible moment Harriet thought the girl would refuse, but to her relief—and everyone else's—Claudia smiled brilliantly at the young man and took his hand to run onto the floor.

'Thank God for that,' said Marcus piously. 'If you have any feeling for me at all, James, dance with her once to-night or she'll give us hell before she goes back to London tomorrow.'

Lily eyed her brother in disapproval. 'Why should he? It's James's party; he should do what he likes.'

James beckoned David over for a word, and the young man nodded and went off.

'Something wrong, James?' asked Moira.

'No. I just sent instructions to the band to cater for the younger element from now on.'

'Anyone would think you were Methuselah, James,' she protested.

'When it comes to this kind of thing I feel like it,' he said dryly, and sat back to watch as the band thumped into the latest chart-topper. The small dance floor was imme-diately packed with heaving bodies as Lily and Dominic raced off to join Claudia and Tom. But eventually Claudia became the centre of a group with no partners required as she danced with an abandon which drew young men around her like bees to a honeypot as she tossed her long blonde locks and from time to time threw triumphant glances towards James to make sure he was watching her.

Aubrey Wilde drained the last of his brandy and stood up. 'Past my bedtime,' he said apologetically as James got to his feet. 'Thank you for a damn fine party, Crawford, but I think I'll cut along now. A great pleasure to meet you both,' he said to the Graveneys. 'Goodnight. Coming, Harriet?'

'Don't worry, sir,' said James. 'I'll see that your daughter gets back to the Lodge safely.' He signalled to David, and the young man accompanied Aubrey from the marquee, chatting pleasantly as they went. 'How about a drink, Harriet? Moira?'

Moira smiled ruefully. 'Right now, I long for a cup of tea.'

'If you fancy a short walk I can provide you with some at the Lodge,' Harriet offered.

'I can provide it here,' said James, and beckoned to a waiter. 'Tea, Marcus?'

'Not for me, dear boy. I shall just nurse my last brandy while I marvel at the energy of the young!'

Harriet was glad of the tea, but felt suddenly depressed because she felt old and staid to be drinking it instead of bouncing around on the dance floor. She was still, she reminded herself sharply, one whole year short of her thirtieth birthday.

'Something wrong?' said James in her ear.

She smiled ruefully. 'I just feel like a different generation from that lot on the floor.'

'You didn't look it when you were performing that bloody tango,' he said in an undertone.

She turned to look him in the eye. 'You disapproved?'

'Of course I—' He broke off as a piercing scream came from the dance floor. The music stopped and James and Marcus tore down the room with David to push the dancers aside. Moira gasped in horror as they came back flanking Tom with a hysterical Claudia in his arms, Lily in tears following behind with Dominic.

Sweating and breathing hard, Tom set his burden down very carefully next to Moira. She thanked him gratefully, then concentrated on Claudia, her voice soothing as she quietened the girl.

'It was those stupid, stupid heels,' cried Lily hoarsely. 'She turned on her ankle and—and just fell with a horrible thump.'

'Where's the nearest hospital?' demanded Marcus, white to the gills as Claudia's moans rose in anguished crescendo.

'Across town. I'll show you,' said Harriet, thankful she'd kept to one glass of champagne. 'Is your car parked in the paddock?'

James nodded grimly, and beckoned to David. 'Find my driver.'

Harriet shook her head. 'I know the quickest route and my car's right here at the Lodge. I'll bring it to the top of the steps. You'd better stay here and see to your guests, James.'

Harriet could hear James making explanations over the microphone as she ran with Dominic, who insisted on accompanying her to the Lodge. 'I'll just change my shoes before I get in the car,' she gasped.

'It's Claudia's fault! She was like a wild thing on the dance floor. In those heels she was an accident waiting to happen. She ruined James's party.'

Dominic, it was obvious, was not one of Claudia's fans.

'It was just about over, anyway,' Harriet panted as they reached the Lodge. 'I'm fine, Dominic. You go back to Lily.'

'I'll wait until you get in the car,' he insisted.

'In that case, you get in too.' She rushed inside to exchange her heels for flats and swiftly backed her car along the terrace until she was level with the steps leading down to the lawn. 'Leave the passenger doors open, Dominic, and tell the others I'm ready for the off. I'll keep the engine running.'

James carried a moaning, shivering Claudia up to the car, and installed her carefully on the back seat.

'There's a blanket,' said Harriet. 'She'll need it.'

'Thanks,' he said tersely, and turned to help his sister in beside Claudia. Moira wrapped the girl gently in the blanket and held her close, smiling in reassurance at her husband as he got in beside Harriet.

'We'll soon get her sorted, Marcus.'

Claudia turned her face into Moira's shoulder and wept bitterly. 'I spoiled...everything...for James.'

'No, you didn't,' he said briskly. 'It was nearly time for the party to break up, anyway. I'll follow on as soon as I can.' He looked at Harriet. 'Thanks for this.'

'Only too happy to help,' she assured him, and took off along the terrace and down the familiar winding bends to the road, hoping there hadn't been an influx of Saturday night accidents at the hospital. Fortunately, the emergency department was relatively quiet for once when Harriet ran inside to request a wheelchair, and Claudia was eventually assessed, then X-rayed, and finally wheeled off to have her ankle put in plaster, with Moira and Marcus in close attendance. Soon afterwards James arrived with Lily and

Dominic, and Harriet, shivering by this time in spite of the hospital's heat, was able to go home.

Lily hugged her gratefully. 'Thank you for everything. I was running around like a headless chicken, and you were so cool and organised.'

'Was it just a sprain?' said James.

Harriet shook her head. 'Broken, I'm afraid.'

'Hell. She would wear those insane heels. You're cold,' he added, and took off his jacket. 'Here, put this on.'

She shook her head. 'Don't need it. I'm off home now.'

'Dammit, woman, put it on, you're shivering,' he growled, and put it round her shoulders.

'I'll see you to your car,' offered Dominic.

'No need. I'll do that,' said James brusquely.

Harriet was so glad of the jacket in the cold, eddying wind outside she was sorry to hand it over to James as they reached her car. 'I'll be fine now. Goodnight.'

His face was stern in the harsh car park lighting as he looked down at her. 'The marquee people will be at the house in the morning to dismantle the thing, so you can't even have a peaceful stay in bed. You were a great help tonight, Harriet. None of us could have organised the trip to hospital so quickly.'

'No trouble for me. I'm a local. I'm sorry your party ended like that, James. Otherwise it was a triumph.' She looked him in the eye. 'So come on, tell me the truth. Was your revenge sweet?'

He shook his head. 'Not really.'

'You mean it's incomplete. Never mind, my father will soon know who you are. I must go,' she added, shivering. 'Goodnight, James.'

'Your teeth are chattering. Get in a hot bath before you go to bed, and have a good rest tomorrow.'

'If you tell me I look tired I'll get violent and *you'll* be in the emergency room!'

'You look gorgeous, and you know it. God knows there were enough men hovering around to convince you,' he said grimly. 'David was bowled over, and so, I suspect, is young Dominic. But leave him alone, please, he belongs to Lily.'

'Are you serious?' Harriet stared at him in utter disgust. 'I'm not into cradle-snatching.'

'What are you into these days? This?' He jerked her into his arms and kissed her with a violence she responded to helplessly, her mouth parting to the insistence of his as his arms locked her in an embrace which was so familiar and right she melted against him, her heart hammering against his as his arms tightened. When she finally regained wits enough to try to free herself he let her go and stood back, his breathing laboured as he glared down at her. 'Do you want me to apologise?'

She glared back and got in the car without a word, leaving him staring after her as she drove away.

CHAPTER SIX

IT TOOK Harriet the entire drive home to calm down. She locked the Lodge door behind her at last and trudged upstairs to hang up the dress, surprised to see it had survived the adventures of the night remarkably well, including the sudden, volcanic embrace that marked the end of it. She shivered, her teeth chattering again at the thought of it, and stood under a hot shower before falling into bed.

She woke next morning to find a couple of extra hours in bed had proved possible after all. The marquee crew didn't arrive until mid-morning. Harriet made herself some strong coffee, then with reluctance rang James to ask after Claudia.

'She's full of painkillers and fast asleep right now,' he informed her. 'How are you, this morning, Harriet?'

'A bit tired,' she said brightly. 'Otherwise, I'm fine.'

'I was just about to drive up to your place to make sure the marquee people had left everything in good order. Are they still there?'

'They've only just arrived.'

'Right. I'm on my way.'

Harriet clenched her teeth, and told herself to stop behaving like an idiot. James was just coming to make sure there was no damage he had to pay for. In the meantime she'd better tell her father about Claudia's accident. She caught him just as he was backing his car out of the garage.

'Can't stop,' Aubrey said hastily. 'Did you enjoy the party, Harriet?'

'I did. But you missed all the excitement.' She gave him the details but, although he made suitable exclamations of shock and sympathy, he was obviously impatient to leave. Duty done, Harriet went back to the Lodge and with a sigh of pleasure curled up on her sofa with the Sunday papers and a mug of coffee. Shortly afterwards she heard the Aston Martin coming up the drive and took in a deep, calming breath as she opened the door to James. He looked tired and very dark under the eyes, his smile wry as he handed her a sheaf of flowers.

'These are from Moira and Marcus to show their gratitude for your help last night. I told them it would be coals to Newcastle in this place, but they insisted, so I found a garden centre.'

'How lovely. Please thank them for me. Is Claudia still sleeping?'

'She was when I left, thank God.' His mouth turned down. 'Let's hope she stays that way for a while to give Moira a break. Put these in water and come outside to check the garden with me. Please,' he added irritably when she made no move to obey.

Harriet's lips twitched as she went into the kitchen. A little dressage now and again had always been good in her dealings with James. During their relationship he'd had a tendency to take over too much, but back then she'd been too hopelessly in love with him to mind.

'Good,' he approved, as she locked her door behind her. 'You need to be security conscious in a big property like this. Does living so far from the main house ever bother you?'

'Never. For me it's the main advantage,' she assured him.

James frowned down at her as they walked up the drive. 'As I've said before, you've changed a lot, Harriet.'

'After all this time it would be strange if I hadn't! You've changed a lot yourself, James.'

'Not in the ways that matter,' he said shortly, and raised an eyebrow. 'Should we ask your father to come with us?'

She shook her head. 'He's out. Father leads a hectic social life.'

They paused at the head of the steps to watch the efficient dismantling process.

'I didn't see any vehicle as I came up,' remarked James.

'They came via the paddock.' Harriet turned away. 'I'll leave you to it.'

'Going out?'

'No. I've got a date with a sofa and the Sunday papers.' She gave him the polite smile that so obviously irritated him.

James nodded brusquely. 'I'll just repeat my thanks for your help last night. As a matter of interest, did you enjoy the party?'

'Far more than I expected. Your people obviously had a great time. It was a party to remember.' She felt her colour mount as his eyes speared hers.

'Unforgettable in more ways than one!' He heaved in a deep breath. 'I'm driving Claudia back to London after lunch. She's feeling so rough she wants her mother. Marcus is due in court first thing tomorrow, so I volunteered to get the invalid home to Mummy and take Lily and Dominic with me.' He stretched, yawning. 'Tomorrow I get back to the Live Wires grindstone. How about you?'

'I get back to my particular grindstone, too,' Harriet said cheerfully. 'Convey my thanks for the flowers, and wish Claudia a quick recovery. Goodbye, James.'

'Keen to get rid of me?' he said dryly.

'Not at all. I assumed you were in a hurry to get back to your family.'

He frowned. 'Speaking of family, let me know if your father cuts up rough when he finds out about me.'

'What could you possibly do?'

James shrugged. 'Provide a shoulder to cry on?'

'I've learnt to do without one of those, but thanks for the thought.' Harriet turned away, assuming he wanted to talk with the marquee crew, but James saw her back to the Lodge.

'Moira likes you, Harriet,' he said abruptly as she unlocked her door. 'She doesn't know anyone here yet, so when she asks you to the Old Rectory again, would you go? I'm not likely to be there for a while, if that makes a difference.'

'I'm happy to visit your sister any time. Whether you're there or not.' Harriet held out her hand. 'Goodbye, James.'

He shook it briefly. 'Make it *au revoir*. I'm likely to be around quite often now Moira lives here.'

Harriet eyed him curiously. 'You know, there was one thing I never found out all those years ago, James. What brought you to this part of the world in the first place?'

'Work. I applied for the job Combe Computers advertised, and the rest, as they say, is history. Now, it's time I was off to let you recharge those batteries of yours.' He smiled. 'Unless you'd like some help with that?'

Harriet's eyes narrowed. Was he actually thinking of picking up where he'd left off last night?

His eyes gleamed. 'Don't worry; I wasn't asking to share your bed for some afternoon delight. Not,' he added, moving nearer, 'that the idea lacks appeal.'

She backed away. 'How flattering.' She gave him her best social smile and went into the Lodge, shutting the door behind her with a decisive click.

James stood staring at the closed door for a moment, and then strode off to consult with the marquee crew. Once he was satisfied there would be nothing left behind to mar the perfection of the River House grounds he got back in his car. One thing was obvious, he realised, as he negotiated the steep bends of the drive, last night's triumph had not been quite enough to satisfy him after all. Their waltz together had been a subtle form of purgatory for him, and watching her dance that sexy tango afterwards had added fuel to the flame. Miss Wilde was mistaken if she thought everything was over. Besides, he thought with sudden satisfaction, Aubrey Wilde still had to discover who, exactly, had provided the money he'd been so eager to accept.

CHAPTER SEVEN

HARRIET spent the next day in a series of sessions with clients, and arrived home wanting nothing more than a shower, supper and bed. Instead she found a message from her father on her phone, demanding her presence up at the house. She heaved a sigh. It was show time!

Instead of rushing off straight away, Harriet washed her face, renewed her make-up and re-coiled her hair even more tightly than usual. Armour firmly in place, she marched up to the house and found her father in the kitchen, waiting to pounce.

'So there you are at last!' he stormed, his face suffused with rage. 'I suppose you're satisfied now you've made a bloody fool of me, Harriet! You actually had the gall to persuade me to let that man hire my house under false pretences. All those years ago you refused to give me your lover's name, but George Lassiter took great pleasure today in telling me the truth.'

'He's James Crawford, just as he always was,' she retorted, her response so different from the girl he'd bullied ten years before that Aubrey Wilde blinked cautiously and backed off. 'He didn't give you a false name, and he is the head of the Live Wires Group—also the man you would have had arrested merely for daring to like your daughter.'

'Like!' He snorted. 'He wanted you to shack up with him, so I bet he did more than just 'like' you.'

'Don't judge everyone by your own standards, Father,' she snapped.

'What the hell do you mean by my standards?' His eyes slid away. 'If you're referring to Mrs Fox, we're just good friends.'

Mrs Fox? Who was she? 'I'm not interested in your relationship with the lady, whoever she is. I'm talking about my mother.'

Aubrey turned crimson. 'I suppose Miriam's been pouring poison in your ears—'

'Is it poison or the simple truth? She told me exactly why your reaction to my relationship with James was so extreme all those years ago.' Harriet's relentless eyes held his. 'You were so determined to marry Miss Sarah Tolliver and live the good life here at River House you made sure of her in the time-honoured way. No wonder you took it for granted James was after the same thing with me.'

Aubrey Wilde's eyes bulged, veins stood out on his neck as he stood with hands clenched, and for a moment he looked about to collapse.

Harriet advised him to sit down. 'You don't look well, Father.'

He gave her a look that should have felled her on the spot. 'If I'm not you're to blame. Miriam, too, curse the woman. Sarah told her everything, always, but Miriam swore she would never say a word—'

'But the word she did say was the truth, wasn't it? In her opinion, you would have done anything to marry Mother and live here at River House, which is exactly what you did. Grandfather was forced to accept you, use his influence to get you a promotion at the bank.'

'I gained that by my own merit!' he roared, his colour high again. 'Miriam's a viper, always has been. Frank Cairns was a saint to put up with her.'

'He loved her,' said Harriet simply. 'That's the usual reason for people to marry. I loved James, too—'

'You were too young to know your own mind.'

She smiled scornfully. 'I was nineteen—the same age as Mother when you married her.'

Aubrey Wilde's fists clenched. 'If you loved Crawford that much, why didn't you have the guts to run away with him?'

'Because you threatened to have him arrested! I loved him too much to risk ruining his life.'

'I wouldn't have gone that far,' he muttered, eyes falling. 'Just getting him fired was enough, because it took him away from you.'

'Actually, he wasn't fired. Mr Lassiter merely transferred him up north to another branch of the firm. James was too good at his job to lose—as he's proved beyond all doubt.'

'And I thought George was my friend!' Aubrey eyed her bitterly. 'No doubt you and Crawford were laughing behind my back all evening.'

'Absolutely not.' She smiled bleakly. 'James is no fonder of me than he is of you. He thinks I dumped him because he wasn't good enough for Miss Harriet Wilde of River House, but he waited a long time before he found the perfect way to retaliate.'

Aubrey glared at her in frustration. 'I'll refund his damned money—'

'You know perfectly well that isn't possible, Father. You signed a contract. Besides, most of the money is already in the business account, and I flatly refuse to give it back.'

She shrugged. 'James can crow over us as much as he likes as long as I get the roof repaired.'

He shook his head, depressed now. 'You used to be such a biddable child—'

'Any personality change is down to you,' she informed him bluntly.

He winced. 'If you felt like that, why the hell did you take a job here when you qualified? I'm sure it wasn't to please *me*!'

'No, it was to please Mother. I promised her I'd make sure you took care of the house.'

'When did you promise her that?'

'When she was dying.'

'I didn't know about it.'

'You weren't around much at the time.'

'I couldn't bear to watch her fading away.' He glared at her through sudden tears and scrubbed at them with a handkerchief. 'You forgot your promise fast enough when you wanted to run off with Crawford!'

'I wasn't leaving the country! I was a teenage student, Father, and at the time you were financially stable. I took it for granted that you would care for River House because it was our home.'

He blew his nose irritably. 'The home you moved out of the minute you qualified. After I saved you from ruining your life you couldn't bear to stay under the same roof with me.'

She nodded. 'Pretty much. Though it's unlikely I would have ruined my life by sharing it with a man who went on to make such a spectacular success of his own.'

'How was I to know that at the time? I thought he was just some upstart wanting to get a foot in the door here at River House.'

'As you did with Mother,' Harriet said mercilessly. 'But,

unlike you, James wasn't interested in River House. He just wanted me.' She turned to go. 'By the way, I had an email from Charlotte Brewster today. Apparently she has someone else in line for an event here. She's popping into my office tomorrow to discuss it. I'll keep you informed.'

'Harriet!'

She turned back. 'Yes?'

'Is Crawford likely to come here again?'

'No. Now the party's over he'll have no reason to.'

Aubrey sighed again. 'Life plays some strange tricks. Now I've met him I like the man; his family, too. I just wish—'

'Too late, Father.' Harriet smiled coldly. 'James achieved revenge in his own peculiar way, and that's that. End of story.'

Harriet went back to the Lodge feeling wrung out. She'd been shaping up for this confrontation for so long it was hard to believe she'd finally said all the things she'd been bottling up. Not that they'd make any difference. Her father would go on tomorrow as though nothing had happened, as he always did. While she felt sick with reaction, and no longer sure she was doing the right thing. Maybe it was time to move on, apply for a job somewhere else, and leave her father to face up to his responsibilities at last.

Harriet slept so badly that Lydia took one look at her next morning and sent Simon off to make coffee before she began her day.

Charlotte Brewster, prompt as usual, informed Harriet she was following up more queries regarding River House. 'One is from a firm that makes luxury beds. They want a romantic bedroom with big windows, so the large one with the balcony would be the perfect choice. But they might

want to paint the walls a different colour. Would your father be up for that?'

'I'm sure he would. What else have you got?'

Harriet's mood improved considerably at the news that
the rock group currently at the top of the charts might use
the house for a music video, and a television company was
interested in using the house and garden for scenes in a
forthcoming drama series.

'In the meantime,' said Charlotte, 'houses like yours are
constantly sought after as venues for PR events, product
launches and commercial photo shoots, so there could be
good pickings for you on a regular basis.'

'Julia said she might be able to help in the photo shoot
area.'

'Give her my number and tell her to get in touch, and
we'll sort it.' Charlotte grinned. 'What did she think of her
family home as the venue for James Crawford's bash last
Saturday?'

'She was all for it.'

'Did you enjoy it?'

'I hadn't expected to, but yes, I did.' Harriet smiled
wryly. 'I put in an appearance to make sure that nothing
untoward happened, but I needn't have bothered. It was a
very classy operation. No expense spared to make it a success.'

Life felt rather flat for a while after the party. Harriet saw
nothing of her father, who kept well out of her way after
their showdown. James rang twice, but she was out on both
occasions and he didn't ring again. She went out to dinner
with friends one night and at the weekend to a concert in
the town hall with Nick Corbett, and spent both evenings
answering questions about the party.

'You know, Harriet,' Nick said, eyeing her, 'I hardly recognised you in the shot in the paper.'

She smiled demurely. 'I clean up well when I try.'

On the way out after the concert Harriet spotted a familiar face and intercepted Moira Graveney. 'Hello there! Did you enjoy the concert? You remember Nick Corbett?'

'Of course, we met at the King's Head. Good evening, Mr Corbett. Harriet, how lovely to see you!' Moira smiled warmly, the familiar hazel eyes alight with pleasure. 'I enjoyed the music very much. I love Mozart, but Marcus doesn't, so I came on my own.'

'How is Claudia?'

'Mending slowly. Her main problem is boredom.'

'She broke her ankle at the party,' Harriet informed Nick.

'Bad luck!' he said, wincing. 'Ladies, will you excuse me for a moment—a friend is beckoning.'

'I'm so glad I ran into you, Harriet,' said Moira. 'I was going to ring you tomorrow to ask if you'd come to lunch next Sunday. Unless you've had rather too much of my family lately?'

'No, indeed,' Harriet assured her. 'I'd like that very much.'

'Come about twelve. If the weather holds we'll eat in the garden.' Moira waved as a familiar figure entered the foyer. 'Ah, my chauffeur's arrived.'

Harriet smiled brightly as James Crawford came towards them.

'You're very punctual, James,' said his sister.

'Would I dare keep my sister waiting? Not that I had much choice; Marcus has been giving me reminders about the time for the past half hour.' He turned to Harriet. 'And how are you?'

'Always better for a dose of Mozart,' she assured him,

and turned as Nick came back. 'You remember Nick Corbett?'

James's nod was cool. 'Of course. You're a Mozart fan too?'

Nick shook his head, smiling. 'Not really. I bought the tickets to please Harriet.'

'Time we were off,' said Moira and, to Harriet's surprise, leaned forward to kiss her cheek. 'Don't forget. Sunday at twelve.'

'I'll look forward to it,' Harriet assured her.

'Good to see you both again,' said James, and took Moira's arm to lead her outside.

'For a busy man he spends a lot of time in this area,' said Nick as they followed suit.

'Because his sister moved here recently. He's very fond of Moira.'

'Is it possible he's fond of you, too?' said Nick with a sidelong glance.

'You couldn't be more wrong,' she assured him.

'Good to know. How about a drink at the King's Head before you go home?'

Harriet enjoyed the drink and a lively chat with Nick in the busy bar and arrived home later to find a message on her machine from James.

'Third time unlucky, it seems. I'll try again some time. Or you could even ring me.'

Not a chance. James might get the mistaken impression that she was trying to rekindle something between them. Maybe he would be at Moira's for lunch next Sunday. Not that she cared whether he was there or not. It would be good just to enjoy a meal and a pleasant hour or two with the Graveneys. It certainly beat the housework and gardening she usually did on Sundays. She had learned her lesson when she made her permanent move into the Lodge.

A small house had to be kept scrupulously tidy. And if she sometimes yearned for the space and light up at the main house she never admitted it to herself, let alone anyone else.

CHAPTER EIGHT

THE following Saturday Harriet was in the middle of attacking the chores usually done on Sunday when she was surprised by a rare phone call from Sophie.

'Harriet—oh, thank God. You're there. Can you do me a huge favour? Please, please, say you will or I'll—'

'Whoa! Is something wrong with Annabel?'

'Yes, no—I mean—'

'Take a deep breath and calm down. What's wrong?'

'Gervase has just driven Pilar to the airport. We've been invited to a garden party tomorrow, and Pilar's had to rush off to Spain today for some family crisis—so inconsiderate, I'm sure she could have waited until Monday. There'll be lots of really useful people for Gervase at the party, so he says we've just got to go, but children are not invited, and there's no one to look after Annabel—and—and...' Sophie trailed off into hysterical tears.

'Sophie! For heaven's sake, stop blubbing.' Harriet sighed. Goodbye to lunch with the Graveneys. 'All right, I'll come, but on the strict understanding that you leave the party in good time for me to get back here in the evening. I've got to be in work first thing on Monday, remember.'

'Honestly, Harriet, is work all you can think about...?' Sophie stopped, regrouping hurriedly. 'Sorry, sorry. I'm so upset I can't think straight. So you'll drive over this evening?'

And sleep in Annabel's room so the child didn't disturb her mother in the night now Pilar wasn't there! 'No, I can't, sorry.'

'Surely you can put off what you have on tonight,' wheedled Sophie. 'Please, Harriet.'

'Look, Sophie, I had a lunch invitation myself tomorrow. I'm willing to cancel that to help you out, but I'm not driving over to you tonight. I'll come in the morning.'

'Oh. Oh, all right. But make sure you come in good time tomorrow; we're due at the party at twelve.'

It was absurd, Harriet informed herself, to feel so disappointed. Apparently she'd been looking forward to Sunday lunch with the Graveneys more than she'd let herself admit. She shrugged philosophically, and rang Moira to say she couldn't make it.

'My sister has a domestic crisis and needs a babysitter tomorrow. I'm really sorry about this. I hope it hasn't put you out in any way.'

'Not at all. But we were looking forward to seeing you again. Never mind. Families come first.'

'As you well know. How is Claudia?'

'Stir-crazy, according to Lily, though apparently not short of visitors.'

No surprise there! 'Moira, since I can't make it tomorrow, do you fancy having lunch in town with me one day instead?'

'I'd like that very much indeed. When?'

They settled on a date, and Harriet put her phone away feeling marginally happier, but too restless to sit in her now immaculate house on a sunny Saturday afternoon. Tomorrow would be exhausting, so it was only common sense to read a book, watch TV, or simply lie on her sofa and do nothing while she had the chance. Instead, Harriet slapped on sunblock and thrust her hair through the back of a baseball cap, then went up to the big double garage behind the main house to take out the sit-on lawn mower.

Harriet was sweating profusely, her khaki shorts and sleeveless tank top dirty and some of her hair sticking in damp rings on her forehead and neck by the time the big main lawn bore satisfying stripes of newly cut grass. She emptied out the last container of clippings into the area hedged off for compost, and got back on to the machine to drive it out through the shrubbery onto the main drive. Her heart plummeted to her scruffy sneakers at the sight of James leaning against his car, scowling in disapproval as she chugged past him.

'Can't stop,' she yelled. 'Must put this away.'

In an agony of frustration at the machine's slow speed, and horribly aware of his eyes on her sweat-soaked back as he stalked after her, Harriet negotiated the tricky slope with care. When the machine was finally stowed in the vast garage she switched off, slid from the seat and wrenched off her gloves as James cornered her.

'Why in God's name are you slaving away in heat like this?' he said harshly. 'Can't this gardener of yours mow the lawn?'

She took a wad of tissues from her pocket and mopped her face. 'Of course he can, but I do it sometimes to leave him free to do the other stuff. Are you here for the weekend?' she added politely.

'Why have you cancelled tomorrow?' he demanded, ignoring her. 'Were you afraid of running into me again?'

'Of course not,' she said irritably. 'Look, I can't hang about. I need a shower.'

'I'll wait while you clean up,' he said flatly. 'Trying to get in touch with you by phone is so damned frustrating I opted for the personal touch today when Moira said you'd cancelled. Come clean, Miss Wilde. Is there really a family crisis? Or can't you face making polite conversation with me over the roast?'

Harriet marched down the drive to the Lodge beside him, furious because he'd surprised her when she was dirty and sweaty, and probably didn't smell too wonderful at close quarters. 'Do you want to come in?' she said ungraciously, and kicked off her shoes in the porch.

'I said I'd wait,' he reminded her. 'But if you'd rather I didn't come in I can sit in the car.'

'Don't be ridiculous!' She went ahead of him into the house and ran upstairs at breakneck speed.

When Harriet eventually went down to the sitting room her uninvited guest was stretched out on the sofa watching cricket on her television. James got to his feet as she joined him.

'I hope you don't mind. It was the last few overs of the day.'

'Not at all.'

'Do you feel better now, Harriet?'

She nodded.

His eyes narrowed as he took in her yellow cotton dress. 'You had a dress like that years ago.'

She'd worn it the first time they went out together. 'Really? I don't remember.'

'Don't you?' James met her eyes in a challenge Harriet chose to ignore.

'I'm thirsty, I need a drink. Would you like one? No beer or wine, but I can give you mineral water, orange juice, tea, coffee…'

'Anything—' he broke in '—whatever's easiest.'

When Harriet got back with two glasses of mineral water James was standing at the window, frowning. 'All those trees and flowers out there in the gardens, yet all you can see from here is a strip of lawn and a high laurel hedge.'

'I get a good view of the gardens from my bedroom,' she said defensively, and handed him a glass.

He turned a hostile look on her. 'I wouldn't know. Bedrooms never featured in our relationship. And you never let me come back here again after the first day I came to mend your computer.' His deep voice grew harsh. 'Like a fool I allowed you to treat me like a dirty secret all that summer because I thought everything would be different once we had a place together. But it never happened.'

'No,' she agreed stonily. 'It didn't.'

'And why the hell can't you afford a bottle of wine?' James demanded irritably. 'You must earn good money, and you live here rent free—'

'Actually, I don't. I pay rent to my father. And this place is too small to entertain, so keeping wine or whatever for guests isn't necessary—' She broke off as her phone rang, and excused herself to answer Sophie.

'Hi.'

'Thank goodness I've caught you. Harriet, be a darling. Please put off your date, or whatever, and come this evening. Annabel is so looking forward to seeing you, and it would be much more convenient—'

'For you, maybe, but not for me. Tell Annabel I'll be there in the morning.'

'Oh, all *right*!' snapped Sophie. 'Just make sure you get here in good time.'

'I'll *be* there.'

Harriet closed her phone with a snap. 'Sorry. That was my sister.'

James raised an eyebrow. 'The hotshot journalist or the spoilt pretty one?'

'The latter. Sophie is still pretty, still spoilt, but now married to the man she met at a wedding.'

'Who is Annabel?'

'My niece. Sophie's au pair had to make a sudden trip home to Spain today. Annabel's parents are invited to some vitally important social event tomorrow so I'm looking after her.' Harriet smiled as she took the window seat. '*That's* why I'm missing lunch at the Old Rectory, James Crawford. Moira is lunching with me in town this week instead.'

The cold eyes warmed as he returned the smile. 'So she told me. She's looking forward to that.'

'Me too. By the way, I gather Claudia is progressing well, but very bored. Have you seen her lately?'

'I called in recently for a few minutes. I was in London for a dinner and went to see her next day on my way home.' He gave her a wry smile. 'Lily and Dominic were there, plus a couple of girlfriends and a rather embarrassed Tom Bradfield. My presence put such a damper on the occasion I didn't stay long. According to Lily, Tom drives down to see Claudia regularly since the accident.'

Harriet's eyes sparkled. 'Cutting you out, James?'

'Looks like it, thank God,' he muttered.

'Shouldn't you let Claudia know that? She has a huge crush on you, James.'

'Had, maybe; not any more. Anyway, my feelings towards her—and to Lily—have always been brotherly.'

'Oh, come *on*. You weren't very fraternal that night at the Old Rectory!' she scoffed.

James reddened. 'I had cause to regret that later when Moira hauled me over the coals.'

Harriet looked at him steadily. 'I knew, as soon as I got to the Old Rectory, why I was there. I could have given you the necessary information on the phone, but you wanted me to see you in your family setting, with a gorgeous creature like Claudia panting after you.'

He winced. 'Sounds really immature put like that, but I can't deny it. That day in your office you were so remote and haughty behind your desk I seized on the chance of showing you I'd come a long way from the computer techie who wasn't good enough for Miss Harriet Wilde of River House.'

'I never thought of you that way,' she said flatly.

'But your father did.'

She bit her lip. 'I'm afraid so. But only because he'd never met you—'

'Not my fault.'

'I know.' She looked away. 'I wanted to keep you to myself, so nothing spoiled what we had together.'

'But when you told him you were joining forces with me, that was it.'

She nodded. 'Father put his foot down.'

He smiled sardonically. 'Your father could hardly have locked you up and kept you on bread and water, Harriet. You could have left home if you'd really wanted to. Was it a matter of money? You couldn't have made it through college without his support?'

She was tempted to take the easy way out and say yes. She shook her head. 'I had a college fund from my mother for that.'

James's eyes darkened. 'Then why the hell didn't you just take off with me?' he demanded, his voice roughening. 'Were you afraid I'd want a share of the fund?'

'No, James,' she said wearily. 'Is this why you came here today, to rake over past history?'

'No. Believe it or not, I thought you might be ill.' His mouth twisted. 'Instead I found you careering round on that blasted machine in this heat. And tomorrow you'll be running round after your sister's child all day. How old is she?'

'Three.'

'Do you often drop everything to look after her?'

'Only in times of crisis.' Harriet smiled wryly. 'Though Sophie's idea of a crisis usually differs from mine. She's always been a drama queen.'

'You don't get on well?'

She shrugged. 'She's jealous of me because I'm the one at home with Father.'

James frowned. 'And yet you're the one she calls on in an emergency.'

'I live a mere hour away by car and Julia's based in London.' Harriet grinned suddenly. 'Not that Sophie would have any luck with Julia anyway. She's not exactly the babysitting type.'

'And you are.'

'Yes. A day in Annabel's company is a pleasure, not a chore.'

'Actually, I had another reason for invading your ivory tower,' he informed her.

Her eyebrows rose. 'Not much of a tower, James!'

'The place serves the same purpose. It's where you hide away from the world.'

'I don't hide,' she denied.

His eyes locked on hers. 'So if a man wants to take you to bed it's always his place, not yours.'

'More or less,' she said evenly. 'How about you? I haven't asked where you live these days.'

'I bought a house near Cheltenham a couple of years back. I've been doing it up gradually. The place is listed, so I have to go carefully.' James frowned. 'By the way, does your father know who I am yet?'

'He certainly does. Mr Lassiter took great pleasure in

enlightening him.' Harriet drank the rest of her water. 'Father was so furious I was afraid he'd have a stroke at one point. He ranted and raved for quite a while, but in the end the storm just petered out.' She smiled grimly. 'The really ironic part is that he liked you, and your family. In some ways I think that was the worst thing when he found out who you were.'

James eyed her with sympathy. 'A rocky relationship with your father must be tough. My parents died relatively young, but Dan and I were lucky, of course, because we had Moira.'

'Very lucky.' Harriet sighed. 'I'm really sorry I'll miss her lunch tomorrow. I shall think of you with envy when I'm eating fish fingers and baked beans.'

'Only then?' His eyes were suddenly intent.

'No, indeed. I shall think of you every time I write a cheque for the roofing men!'

'I saw the scaffolding when I parked the car. When do they finish?'

'Next week. And I'm holding them to that because my sister's organising a fashion shoot for her magazine, and later on a television company wants to do some interior scenes for a play.' Harriet smiled brightly. 'You started the ball rolling with your party so your revenge plan backfired a bit, James. You've given River House a new lease of life.'

James dumped his glass down and jerked her into his arms. 'Don't you ever think of anything except this damned house of yours?' He kissed the mouth that opened to protest, his arms crushing her ribs so fiercely she couldn't breathe. The kiss was such pure punishment she lost her temper and bit his tongue, and James cursed and let her go.

Harriet made blindly for the kitchen and tore off a length of kitchen paper. She scrubbed her mouth with some of it and took the rest to James. 'Here,' she said coldly. 'You're bleeding.'

He pressed the wad of paper to the tip of his tongue, eyeing her over it with rancour. 'All you had to do was say no.'

'If I could have spoken I would have,' she snapped. 'What was all that for again, James? Wasn't it enough retaliation to use the house?'

'For God's sake, stop talking about the *house*. The house you don't live in, won't inherit, yet spend your life working yourself into the ground just to keep it ticking over. When are you going to take life by the throat and live it, Harriet?' His eyes held an almost feral glitter. 'This is all we get, and it's short—hell, what's the use?' He took in a deep breath, his manner suddenly formal. 'My apologies.'

'Accepted,' she snapped, then turned sharply as she reached the door. 'I make no apologies for biting you.'

'You've developed violent tendencies with maturity,' he observed as he passed her to go outside. 'Are you like this with all your men?'

'The occasion never arises. They treat me with respect,' she said loftily.

His eyes lit with an unholy gleam. 'How boring! Goodbye, Harriet.'

Too full of warring emotions to trust her voice, she shut the door on him without a word, then gave a shriek as the door suddenly flew open and James took her in his arms to kiss her again, but this time with all the old persuasive magic she had never found with any other man. Against her will, she felt every nerve and sinew responding to his touch until suddenly she was free as he released her.

'That's my real apology,' he said huskily, and left her standing motionless as he flung away. He turned in the doorway. 'Just for the record, if you cried off from Moira's lunch to avoid me you needn't have bothered. I won't be there.'

Harriet stared at the door he closed behind him as she slumped down on the sofa, feeling as though her energy supply had been cut off at the mains. The housework and gardening would have been tiring enough without the turbulent episode with James. Tears burned her eyes and leaked in a salty trail down her flushed face. Damn James Crawford and his kisses. Now he was back in her life again, hard-won acceptance of her lot was hard to maintain.

CHAPTER NINE

THINGS got off to a bad start the next day. Harriet's car refused to start, her father was out, the garage she used wasn't open on a Sunday and she was forced to take a very expensive taxi to get to the large, ultra-modern Barclay home in Pennington. She arrived to a mixed reception—friendly and welcoming from Gervase, impatient from Sophie, and no sign of Annabel, who usually launched herself at her aunt the moment Harriet was through the door.

'You've cut it terribly fine,' Sophie complained. 'It's half past eleven!'

'The car wouldn't start. I had to take a taxi. Where's Annabel?'

Sophie's eyes flickered. 'Sleeping. She's got a bit of a cold.'

'More than a bit; she's got a temperature.' Gervase eyed his wife uneasily. 'I'm not sure you should go out and leave her, darling.'

Sophie stiffened. 'Not go? Why? It's just a cold, and Harriet is more than capable of looking after her. She's good with Annabel.' She turned on her sister. 'You don't mind if I go, do you?'

'No.' Privately, Harriet was amazed that Sophie would want to leave Annabel if the child was unwell. 'Are you going far?'

'Just a short walk away; we could be back in minutes if you need us,' said Gervase, and kissed her cheek. 'Thank you for helping us out, Harriet.'

Sophie had the grace to look contrite. 'Yes, indeed. Though I was afraid you weren't going to make it in time.'

'In which case we would have arrived at the party fashionably late,' said her husband. 'I shall reimburse you for the taxi when we get back, Harriet.' Gervase Barclay, tall, heavily built, elegantly suited, and twenty years older than his wife, looked exactly what he was, a successful businessman very comfortable in his own skin.

His wife, however, was not. Sophie frowned down at herself in doubt. 'Do you think this dress is right for a garden party, Harriet?'

Harriet thought it was wrong for any party. The print was eye-wateringly bright, and the dress too short. 'It looks very summery—'

'You think it's awful—I knew it!' Sophie wailed. 'You'll have to wait, Gervase, while I change.' She took off for the stairs at a run.

'Check on Annabel,' her husband called after her, and smiled ruefully at Harriet. 'Sophie was shattered when Pilar had to leave so suddenly.'

'Family crisis?'

'Her mother's ill. Sophie's lost without Pilar, especially now Annabel's off colour—all three of us had a wretched night. We'll be back by four at the latest, but if you want us earlier, don't hesitate to ring. Here's my mobile number.' He handed Harriet a card, wincing at the sound of sobbing from upstairs.

'You go. I'll see to Annabel.' Harriet ran upstairs to the child's room and found Sophie, now in ice-blue linen and pearls, trying to calm her little daughter.

'Don't cry, darling,' Sophie pleaded frantically. 'Look! Auntie Harriet's come to play with you.'

The child held supplicating arms up to Harriet. 'Want to come down,' she sobbed.

'Then you shall.' Harriet picked her up, alarmed by the child's body heat. 'Let's wash your face first, and then we'll cuddle up on the sofa in the snug. Say goodbye to Mummy.' Behind the child's back she made shooing motions as Sophie pointed to the bottle on the bedside table.

'Give her some of that after her lunch.'

'Don't—want—lunch,' hiccupped the child, burrowing against Harriet's neck.

'I left lots of things in the fridge, but if she doesn't fancy solids just give her fruit,' said Sophie. 'Be good for Auntie, darling.' She dropped a kiss on her child's damp hair, and rushed off.

Harriet collected a nightdress and took her unhappy little niece into the bathroom. She washed the small hot face and sticky hands, and put the fresh nightie over Annabel's head. 'There. You'll feel better now,' she said cheerfully.

Annabel sniffed hard. 'Pilar went home to her poorly mummy, Auntie. Will she come back?'

'Of course she will.' Harriet devoutly hoped so. Pilar was the rock in her niece's life, which was unfair to Sophie, but nevertheless true. Sophie adored her child, but was less fond of the more demanding parts of motherhood, as in getting up in the night and keeping Annabel amused.

Harriet found the bunny slippers Annabel wanted, and took her downstairs to the vast magazine-illustration kitchen. She put the child into her special chair, had a look in the fridge and found a very tempting salad obviously meant for the babysitter, also several possibilities for the child's lunch. 'What would you like, darling? Pasta? Scrambled eggs?'

'Banana, please,' stated Annabel hoarsely.

Resisting the urge to feel the child's forehead again, Harriet sliced a banana and took the dish over to the table with a small pot of yoghurt. 'There. Can you feed yourself, darling, or shall I help you?'

'You help.' Annabel looked up at Harriet in appeal. 'Can I sit on your lap? My chair's hurting me.'

This was worrying news. 'Of course. In fact, shall we have a little treat and take a tray into the snug, so you can watch one of your DVDs while you eat?'

Annabel brightened. 'On your lap.'

Whatever worked, thought Harriet. With a cartoon film on the television to distract her patient, she managed to feed her half of the banana and a little of the yoghurt, but the process was very slow, and by the time she'd given Annabel a drink the little girl was ready to sleep again.

'Medicine first,' said Harriet firmly, 'then you can have a nap.'

'Down here with you!'

'You bet.'

Annabel shed a few tears before the medicine was safely down, but Harriet settled down with her on the sofa, with book, tissues and water bottle in reach, and breathed a sigh of relief when the little body relaxed against her. She cradled the hot little head against her shoulder and smiled at the next inevitable demand.

'Story, Auntie. Please,' the child pleaded, her voice so hoarse Harriet felt a sharp stab of misgiving. This was surely more than a little cold.

'Once upon a time,' she began softly, 'there were three little girls who lived in a lovely big house by the river...' This was an ongoing saga every time she saw Annabel, and the fictional idyll of happy little girls was the only story the child ever wanted, but this time she fell asleep shortly after Harriet began. The fair head grew heavy, and Harriet abandoned any idea of reading as she held the child safe in a reassuring embrace, trusting in nature's remedy of sleep.

It was the only peaceful interlude of the afternoon.

When Sophie hadn't returned by four Harriet decided to ring the number Gervase had given her, but before she could get out her phone Annabel threw up and it took some time to get the child washed and in a fresh nightie and persuade her to drink some water.

'Let's ask Daddy and Mummy to come home, shall we?'

'Want you to stay, Auntie,' croaked Annabel.

'Let's get Mummy and Daddy home, then we'll see, darling.'

When Harriet spoke to Gervase, he was remorseful. 'Lord, I'm sorry, Harriet. We should have left long before now. I'll round up Sophie right away. It's a fair little walk, but we'll be as quick as we can.'

Thinking of Sophie's towering heels, Harriet took that with a pinch of salt, but to her surprise they arrived soon afterwards and Sophie came rushing into the snug, screeching when she felt Annabel's forehead.

'What were you thinking of?' she accused Harriet. 'Why on earth didn't you ring us sooner?'

'When you hadn't come home by four, as promised, I was just about to do so when Annabel was sick again and I took time to clean her up. You need to call your doctor right now,' said Harriet firmly.

Gervase took out his phone as he hurried in. 'I'll do that.' Sophie tried to pick up Annabel but she clung to Harriet.

'Want Auntie!'

'Well, that's nice, I must say—' Sophie swallowed convulsively and clapped a hand to her mouth as she ran for the door. Gervase rolled his eyes.

'A surfeit of Pimms on top of lobster. I stuck to beer, myself—' He broke off and spoke into the phone, and Harriet sat down again with Annabel.

Gervase thanked someone profusely and closed the phone, raking a hand through his hair distractedly as he looked down at his unhappy little daughter. 'The doctor on call will be here as soon as he can, thank God. Because I wasn't driving for once, I indulged a bit too much to get Annabel to his surgery.' His mouth twisted as he bent to stroke his daughter's damp hair. 'We shouldn't have gone out and left her.'

'Sophie said it was important for you to be there.'

'I was able to do some useful networking, certainly. But hell, none of that mattered as much as Annabel. I wouldn't have left her with anyone else but you, Harriet, Pilar included.'

'Thank you. How did you get here so quickly? You must have run all the way.'

'We got a lift from one of the other guests—which reminds me, I've left him kicking his heels in the drawing room.' He looked up as Sophie returned, looking pale. 'Feeling better?'

'The lobster must have disagreed with me,' she said, bridling at the look he gave her.

'Or you had a drink too many! I did too, which was incredibly irresponsible of both of us when our child is ill.'

'I knew she was all right with Harriet,' said Sophie defensively.

Gervase looked down at the flushed, tearstained face of his daughter. 'But she's not all right, is she? We shouldn't have gone.'

'You said it was important that we did.'

'Important for me, not for both of us. You could have stayed home for once.'

Sophie promptly burst into tears, which started Annabel sobbing again.

'Don't cry, darling,' soothed Harriet. 'Mummy's got a headache and needs to make some tea.' She looked pointedly at Sophie. 'I'd like some, too.'

Sophie's tears dried at the stern look her husband gave her. 'Right,' she said thickly, and patted her daughter's head on the way out. 'Mummy will bring you more juice.'

'Perhaps you could top up our Good Samaritan's drink at the same time,' called her husband.

'Could you take Annabel for a moment, Gervase?' Harriet smiled. 'I need a bathroom break.'

'Oh, God, yes, give her to me.' He stripped off his jacket and took his protesting daughter from Harriet. 'There, there, sweetheart. Auntie won't be long.'

As Harriet passed the drawing room on the way back from the bathroom Sophie came to the door, beckoning to Harriet. 'Come and meet James Crawford, who kindly gave us a lift from the party. James, this is my sister, Harriet Wilde—but then, you know that already,' Sophie added with her tinkling social laugh, then turned as the doorbell rang. 'That must be the doctor. Do excuse me.'

James, elegant in a light linen suit, looked at Harriet in silence for a moment. 'I'm obviously in the way here; I should go. But when you rang your sister was in such a panic I offered to drive them.'

'Of course. Very good of you.'

Gervase hurried in. 'Sorry to interrupt, Crawford, the doctor needs some information from Harriet.'

When Harriet ran into the snug Annabel struggled away from her mother's embrace and held out her arms.

'Don't like the man, Auntie,' she sobbed, and the doctor smiled ruefully.

'My bedside manner isn't working today. I gather you

were looking after Annabel this afternoon, Miss Wilde. What have you given her?'

Sophie handed her unhappy child to Harriet. 'I told you exactly when to give her the medicine. I hope you remembered.'

Harriet shot her a scathing look over the child's head. 'Of course I remembered. Annabel had half a banana and a little yoghurt at twelve-thirty, Doctor, after which I gave her a dose. She slept for a while but woke up coughing. She was restless and clingy all afternoon from them on, and very hot. She complained of tummy ache and said her back hurt. I gave her another dose at four, but shortly afterwards she vomited so I kept to sips of water from then on until her parents arrived home.'

Gervase hurried in to join them, looking every year of his age for once. 'What's wrong with her, Doctor?'

'There's a virus going round with all the symptoms your daughter's presenting. Not much to be done except give her plenty of fluids and keep her as quiet as possible while nature takes its course, I'm afraid.' The weary young man picked up his bag. 'Must get on. Contact the practice tomorrow if you need more help.'

Sophie saw the doctor out and hurried back, eyeing Harriet hopefully. 'Could you stay for a while?'

'Only until Annabel goes to bed. Do you think I could have that tea now, Sophie?'

'Oh, gosh, yes, of course. I'll get it now.'

'Are you sure about this, Harriet?' Gervase looked concerned. 'You're working tomorrow.'

Harriet looked down at the flushed sleeping face on her breast. 'I'll stay until she settles. I really hate that word virus. We depend on antibiotics so much, but in this instance they're useless.'

Sophie looked annoyed when she came back with a tea

tray. 'I took such trouble over the salad I made for you, Harriet, but you haven't touched it.'

'Annabel got so upset if I tried to move I never managed to get to the bathroom, let alone eat anything,' she explained.

'Give her to me,' said Gervase firmly. 'I'll have her while you drink your tea. Sophie, get your sister something to eat.'

'Some of that tempting salad would be good, please,' said Harriet, 'but don't bother bringing it in; I can come to the kitchen.'

'You're the one Annabel wants, obviously, so you'd better stay here,' said Sophie, and flounced out of the room.

'Sophie's suffering from guilt pangs,' sighed Gervase.

As well she might, thought Harriet. She downed a cup of tea, and smiled. 'Gosh, I needed that. Now give her to me. You should get back to your guest.'

Gervase carefully handed the drowsy child over. 'I think I'd better start thinking of a replacement for Pilar,' he said quietly. 'If the mother's very ill she might not come back.'

Sophie gasped in horror as she came in. 'Don't *say* that, Gervase. Annabel will be lost without her. So shall I,' she added mournfully, putting a small tray down beside Harriet.

'Thank you, Sophie.'

'I'll see if Crawford would like another drink,' said Gervase, and hurried from the room.

'I know what you're thinking, Harriet, but Gervase made some important contacts, so it was a very good thing we went to the party,' Sophie said belligerently. 'And, talking of parties, why were we left out of the one at River House?'

Harriet shrugged. 'The invitations were from James Crawford, nothing to do with me, Sophie. Father was keen to go and I went purely to make sure nothing went wrong as far as the house and gardens were concerned. The party was such a success it got a lot of publicity in the press.' She gave her sister a significant look. 'And I now have money for the roof.'

Sophie climbed down instantly. 'Does that mean Daddy won't have to sell?'

'It's a start. Julia is bringing her people down for a shoot soon, and Charlotte Brewster has other things lined up after that, so for the time being the outlook is a bit brighter.'

'Oh, thank God,' sighed Sophie. 'Is Daddy pleased?'

'Delighted,' Harriet assured her. 'This looks delicious, Sophie, but I'd rather we got Annabel to bed before I eat anything.'

'Fine. You go on up and I'll join you once I've had a word with James Crawford.' Sophie eyed her sister speculatively. 'You never mentioned that you'd already met him, by the way.'

'It was such a long time ago I'd forgotten,' said Harriet casually, and carried the sleeping child from the room. 'Be careful you don't disturb Annabel when you come back up, because I need to leave…'

But Sophie was already hurrying across the hall to the drawing room. Harriet mounted the stairs slowly, careful not to disturb her little burden, but the moment she tried to put Annabel down in her pretty bed the child made pitiful little moans of protest. With a sigh Harriet sat down with her in a rocking chair and stroked the tangled curls until Annabel was finally quiet. The child made no protest when she was transferred to her bed at last but Harriet waited a few minutes longer, praying that Sophie would be quiet when she came in. Twenty minutes later there was no sign of her sister so Harriet took one last look at the flushed, sleeping little face and went downstairs to the drawing room, where Sophie was busy pumping James for all the details she could get about the party.

She flushed guiltily as Harriet arrived. 'There you are! Is Annabel asleep now?'

'Yes. But go carefully as you check on her.'

'We will,' said Gervase, smiling remorsefully at Harriet. He took his wife by the hand. 'Excuse us for a moment, Crawford.'

The moment they were alone James led Harriet to a sofa. 'For God's sake sit down; you look exhausted.'

Which meant she was a wreck. Harriet sank back against the cushions gratefully. 'It's been a worrying day. Annabel is very unwell, poor scrap.'

James sat beside her. 'Not my business, of course, but if the child was that ill why did your sister go out and leave her?'

Good question. 'Sophie knew Annabel would be safe with me.'

He looked unconvinced. 'I didn't see your car outside.'

'It wouldn't start this morning,' she said, yawning. 'I came by taxi.'

'In that case I'll drive you home. Or are you staying the night?'

'I can't. I'm seeing a client first thing.' She frowned. 'Look, James, it's very kind of you, but I can't let you make a double journey like that.'

'I won't have to. There's a bed always ready for me at the Old Rectory.' James got to his feet as Gervase came back into the room. 'How's your little girl?'

'Sleeping, thank God. Harriet, could you pop upstairs? Sophie wants a word.'

'Of course.' Harriet smiled politely at James. 'If you're gone before I come back down I'll say goodbye now.'

'I'm in no hurry,' he assured her.

'Good man,' said Gervase, shrewd eyes looking from one to the other. 'Since you're driving, Crawford, how about some coffee?'

In Annabel's room, Sophie touched a finger to her lips and led her sister outside onto the landing. 'Please stay the night, Harriet. I'm going to need some help with Annabel, and you're so good with her.'

'Sorry; I must get back. I've got a meeting with a client first thing in the morning.'

'Your job is more important than helping look after your niece?' demanded Sophie with her usual drama.

'A mere party today was more important to you than staying home with your daughter,' Harriet pointed out. 'Look, Sophie, I love Annabel dearly, but my job is the way I earn my living. I have to go home.'

'Oh, very well, but you'll be lucky to get a taxi to take you that far at this time on a Sunday!' said Sophie petulantly, unaware that her statement made her sister's mind up.

'James Crawford has kindly offered to drive me back,' Harriet told her.

Sophie's eyes widened. 'All that way and back again tonight?'

'No. He'll stay overnight at his sister's house in Wood End.'

'In that case I'd better let you go,' said Sophie reluctantly, and then touched Harriet's hand. 'I am grateful, really. Thank you for looking after Annabel.'

'I won't say I enjoyed it because she was so poorly, but I'm always happy to spend time with her. She's a darling. I'll give you a ring tomorrow to see how she is.'

Harriet took a few minutes in the bathroom to wash her face, had a last peep at her sleeping niece, and then followed her sister downstairs to the drawing room. She smiled brightly at James. 'Sorry to keep you waiting. I'll just collect my belongings.'

Without missing a beat, James turned to Sophie to express his good wishes for her daughter's recovery, shook Gervase's hand, and took charge of Harriet's tote bag.

'So what changed your mind?' he asked as they set off.

'Sophie wanted me to stay the night.'

'A ride home with me was the lesser of two evils?'

She shook her head. 'Not at all—I'm very grateful to you, James.'

'You surprised me by announcing you were ready to leave.'

'You didn't look surprised.'

'I've learned to hide my feelings over the years.'

'So have I,' she said bitterly.

'I could tell that the day I came to your office. You must have been shattered to find I was the man who wanted to hire your house, but you never turned a hair.'

'That wasn't the worst part of the deal,' she assured him. 'When you got up to make a speech at your party, for one horrible moment I thought you were going to tell the world you'd hired River House as a way of humiliating my family.'

He shot an appalled stare at her. 'Good God! Surely you knew me better than that, Harriet?'

'The man I once knew, yes, but I hardly recognised the James I knew in the man you've become.'

'Obviously, if you actually thought I'd subject you to such public humiliation. And quite apart from that, only a fool would ruin the party before it had even started. I may be many things but I'm no fool. At least not any more,' he said, in a tone that tied her stomach in knots. 'For your information, Miss Wilde, the well-being of my workforce is a damned sight more important to me than any half-cocked ideas about revenge.'

The rest of the journey passed in silence so tense after that Harriet could have cried with joy when James turned up the drive to the Lodge.

'Thank you so much for driving me home,' she said, and slid out of the car before he could help her.

'Not at all,' he said distantly, and handed her the tote bag. 'I hope your niece gets better quickly.'

'So do I.' Harriet's hand shook as she unlocked the door. Unable to look up to meet the eyes she knew would be coldly hostile, she muttered goodbye and would have dived inside like a sinner seeking sanctuary but James took her hand.

'Harriet. Let's not part like this.' He drew her into his arms and she leaned against him limply. 'Please promise me you're going straight to bed. You look ready to drop.'

'I am.' She smiled up at him. 'Thank you for bringing me home.'

'Any time,' he assured her. 'Sleep well.'

When the last sound of James's car engine had died away a sudden gurgle from her stomach reminded Harriet that she'd had nothing to eat all day. Common sense nudged her into making toast and tea, which she got down somehow before going upstairs to fall into bed. She slept like the dead and found it hard to get out of bed next morning. Her head ached and she felt thoroughly out of sorts as she rang the garage and asked for the loan of a car when they collected hers. She rang to enquire about Annabel while she waited for a mechanic to arrive, and learned that the doctor had been called back first thing.

'I've arranged for a private nurse,' Gervase said wearily. 'The doctor swears it's just a virus, but at three in the morning I was worried it was something a whole lot worse. Sophie was hysterical with worry.'

Harriet rolled her eyes. No need to tell her that. 'I feel so guilty I couldn't stay to help, but I have meetings today—'

'For God's sake, Harriet, you've no need for guilt,' he said instantly. 'You have a job to do. I can pay for whatever nursing is necessary for Annabel.'

Poor child, thought Harriet. 'Give her my love. Sophie, too. Are you going in today?'

'I must for a while, but only after the nurse gets here. From then on I'll work from home until Annabel is on the mend.'

Monday was never Harriet's favourite day of the week. This one was made particularly difficult by the headache, which persisted through a prolonged meeting first thing with one of her most demanding female clients. In the afternoon a long drive in an unfamiliar car to visit another client made her late getting home, with a headache warming up to full migraine standard. Desperate for a bath and bed, her heart sank when she found Miriam Cairns waiting for her. Sometimes, Harriet thought, as she kissed her, she had regrets about giving Miriam a key to the Lodge.

'Working late again? You look ghastly,' accused her godmother militantly, 'and you didn't return my call yesterday.'

Harriet explained why, and offered to make tea.

'Sit down; I'll make it. And throw a sandwich together.'

'I'm not very hungry, but tea would be good.' Harriet smiled wanly as she loosened her hair. 'Thanks, Miriam.'

For once it was good just to sit there and let someone else take over as Miriam set to work in the small kitchen, though Harriet could have done without the running commentary of complaints about Sophie. When Miriam came back with wafer thin sandwiches and buttered scones as well as tea, Harriet smiled ruefully.

'You're spoiling me!'

'About time someone did. You ought to be eating a good roast dinner, but if you're as tired as you look these might go down more easily,' Miriam said, her voice gruff to hide her concern.

'Your scones always do,' said Harriet, touched. 'I was going to ring you this evening. It was too late by the time I got your message last night—which reminds me; I'd better ring Sophie before I eat.'

'Ring her afterwards, girl.'

'No. I'll do it now.'

Gervase reported that Sophie was lying down and Annabel was much the same, but at least not worse. Fortunately, she liked the excellent paediatric nurse the agency had sent, which was giving her parents some respite.

'That's good. Give her my love. How are *you*, Gervase?'

'Marginally happier now we have professional nursing help.' He sighed. 'One feels so helpless when a child is ill. I can't thank you enough for looking after Annabel yesterday.'

'Only too glad to help. Tell Sophie I rang.' Harriet closed her phone and drank some tea.

'Sophie not available?' asked Miriam acidly.

'She was resting. Fortunately, Annabel likes the nurse they hired.'

Miriam snorted. 'I've never had children, so I can hardly throw stones, but I remember your mother coping with all three of you through all the usual childhood complaints. You'd think Sophie could manage one small girl without paying a nurse. She ought to be on her knees giving thanks for a husband rich enough to indulge her with such luxuries.'

'Mother had Margaret to help,' Harriet reminded her.

'And wonderful help she was. But Sarah was the one who actually nursed you and got up in the night when you cried!'

'True.' Harriet sighed. 'I did think of taking some time off to—'

'Not to look after Annabel?' Miriam shook her head in disbelief. 'Let Sophie look after her own child. Better still, find someone suitable to father one and have a child of your own.' Her eyes gleamed. 'I hear you've been seeing quite a bit of the man who took your father's place at the bank.'

'Have you, indeed! Nick Corbett is just someone pleasant to go out with now and then.'

'Better than nothing, I suppose.' Miriam got up. 'Stay where you are, I can see myself out. By the way, did Aubrey ever discover who actually hired River House?'

'He certainly did. We had a big, big row.'

Belligerence gleamed in Miriam's dark eyes. 'Let me know if he turns nasty on you, and I'll sort him out.'

Harriet shook her head. 'I'd better bring him up to date about Annabel. He dotes on that child.'

'She's a sweet little thing,' allowed Miriam, 'which is a miracle with a mother like Sophie. Aubrey was always too indulgent with that girl.'

'She was such a pretty child.'

'Handsome is as handsome does,' retorted Miriam. 'Eat some of this lot, finish off the tea, then get to bed, dear.'

'I will. Thank you for coming round.' Harriet smiled crookedly. 'It's rather nice, this spoiling thing. I could get used to it.'

Miriam laughed, and surprised Harriet by kissing her goodnight.

* * *

Harriet couldn't, after all, face anything to eat. She took pills, drank tea, then put the tray on the floor and rang her father to leave a message about his granddaughter. Duty done, Harriet stretched out on the sofa. She would get up in a minute and get out of her office clothes…

She woke with a start to the sound of hammering on her door and dragged herself to her feet, head spinning. She took in a deep breath, pushing the hair from her face as she opened the door and found James, city-suited and furious, glaring at her.

She managed a feeble hello before darkness swallowed her. When she opened her eyes she was back on her sofa, staring up into James's face as he yelled at her to snap out of it and wake up.

'Please,' she said faintly. 'Stop shouting—I've got a headache.'

'Amongst other things,' he said grimly, touching her forehead. 'You're hot. What the hell do I do now? I can't leave you here like this. You've obviously caught something from your niece.'

'Of course I haven't, it's much too soon for that,' she retorted, and with care sat up. 'I'm just tired, that's all.' She peered up at him curiously. 'What are you doing here, anyway?'

'I'm going back to Moira's for the night, so I thought I'd check up on you on the way. I wanted to talk to you.' He loomed over her in disapproval as he noticed the food on the tray beside the sofa. 'If this excuse for a meal was your dinner, you obviously haven't touched it.'

'I was about to, but I fell asleep,' she said with dignity. 'Would you like a scone?'

'No,' he said explosively, 'I would not. I want to take you up to your room and make sure you're safe in bed before I leave—' His mouth twisted. 'Don't worry; I'm not suggesting I join you there.'

'I didn't think you were,' she snapped, and got up, willing herself to stand without wavering. 'I am perfectly capable of getting myself to bed.'

'You're still in your working clothes,' he said, eyeing her rumpled suit. 'Overtime again?'

'I had a long drive to meet with a client and got home late, at which point my godmother was waiting here for me, so I didn't get the chance to change. She made me the snack you were so rude about, and told me to go to bed. Which I was about to do when you arrived. Satisfied?' Harriet added irritably.

'No, I'm not. You were totally out of it, woman. If I hadn't knocked—'

'Hammered!'

'The lights were on so I thought I'd make sure you were all right before I left. Which you were not,' he said relentlessly.

'I am now.' She frowned. 'What did you want to talk about?'

'Fate,' he said, startling her.

'Extrapolate.'

'My, what big words you use, Grandma!' He grinned, and suddenly the tension eased and Harriet managed a deep breath for the first time since he'd arrived.

'To start with,' he went on, 'it was fate that led me to Charlotte Brewster when I was researching an unusual venue for my works party. Imagine my reaction when I learned that you were Ms Brewster's accountant and, biggest surprise of all, that River House was a possibility for the party.' James sat on the arm of the sofa, looking down at her.

'No doubt you were euphoric,' she said dryly.

'I felt as though Christmas had come early! It was a minor setback when I called in at the bank and found that your father was no longer in charge. But then I saw you, and knew that you, at least, were still around and probably still living at home with Daddy, which meant I could kill two birds with one stone by hiring your house.' James smiled bitterly. 'Only it didn't turn out quite like that.'

'Because the birds got helpful publicity via your party?'

Diamond-bright hazel eyes bored down into large, weary dark ones. 'And because if revenge is a dish best eaten cold it's proving damned hard for me to swallow.'

Harriet could see he was speaking the truth. She could also feel the heat emanating from his body, and caught a whiff of some kind of cologne blended with James's personal pheromones—a potent, familiar mix that was suddenly too much for her. With a stifled apology she leapt unsteadily to her feet and bolted to the kitchen to heave dryly into the kitchen sink.

A hand reached round her to turn on the cold tap and wet a tea towel. Harriet snatched it and pressed it against her hot, sweating face. 'Nemesis,' she muttered into it, and felt James stiffen behind her.

'Are you delirious?' he demanded as he turned her round.

Harriet emerged from the damp cloth, pushed wet tendrils of hair back from her face and, with great dignity, thanked him, staggered slightly as she tried to stay upright, and assured him she would be fine now. James stared down into her ashen face, then picked her up and made for the stairs.

'What are you *doing*?' she gasped.

'Putting you to bed,' he said through his teeth, and peered in through an open door. 'This is your room?'

Harriet's head spun as James deposited her on her bed,

and she was sucked down into a grey mist. 'James—' she said in sudden desperate appeal.

'I'm here.' He smoothed her hair from her face, then undid her jacket and pulled it from her lax arms. She made no protest when he unbuttoned and removed her shirt, and he felt as though he were undressing a doll by the way she just lay there and let him do as he wanted as he tugged her skirt down. Yet there was nothing sexual about the process. The tenderness he'd felt for the teenage Harriet might have lain dormant through the years, but it came alive again in full force as he undressed her down to her underwear, then tucked her under the covers. He tensed as her arms came up and her dark eyes opened in dazed wonder on his face.

'James?'

'Go to sleep,' he said gruffly and felt every muscle in his body harden as she pulled his face down to hers to kiss him.

'I suppose I'm dreaming again,' she said drowsily as her arms fell away.

Shaken, James stood looking down at her as she turned her face into the pillow. If she was delirious maybe she was coming down with the virus her little niece was suffering from. Or maybe she just needed a good rest. He cursed silently as someone knocked on the Lodge door. If this was the banker boyfriend he'd get rid of him fast before he woke Harriet up. James went silently downstairs and ran to the door to wrench it open just as Aubrey Wilde had raised a hand to knock again.

CHAPTER TEN

THE two men stared at each other in antipathy neither made any attempt to conceal. To James this was the man who'd wrecked his relationship with the only woman he'd ever loved. To Aubrey the tall, dominant man eyeing him with such hostility was the thief who'd stolen something he'd never valued enough until Harriet's love was withdrawn from him.

Aubrey didn't bother with a greeting. 'I need a private word with my daughter.'

'Harriet is in bed. She's ill,' said James stonily. 'I have to go, so it's up to you to make sure the place is secure.'

Aubrey stared in umbrage as James strode to his car and drove off. After a moment's hesitation he went inside and closed the door. He waited for a moment, and then heard movement from upstairs and water running in the bathroom and coughed to announce his presence.

'James?' called Harriet hoarsely, wrapping herself in her dressing gown.

'No, it's me,' her father informed her.

So she had been dreaming. She walked very carefully downstairs. If only her head would stop thumping. 'You got my message, Father?' she asked, peering at him through half-closed eyes.

'Yes. Something wrong with Annabel?'

She nodded carefully. 'She's got some kind of virus, poor darling. I was looking after her yesterday while Gervase and Sophie were at a lunch party.'

'Of course Sophie wouldn't miss a party, even if her child was ill,' said Aubrey in disgust. 'Where was her au pair?'

'Pilar had to rush home to Spain, Father,' Harriet said wearily.

'So what's happening now? Is Gervase helping Sophie look after Annabel?'

'He's hired a paediatric nurse.'

'Good God!' Aubrey shook his head in disbelief. 'He's a good man, but a sight too indulgent with Sophie.' He shot a worried look at Harriet. 'You don't look well at all. You should go back to bed.'

For once Harriet was in complete agreement with her father. 'I just came down for some drinks, so now I'll get to bed and stay there.'

Her father's mouth tightened. 'Crawford opened your door to me. What was he doing here?'

Harriet swallowed. So she hadn't been imagining things. 'He was at the same party as Sophie and Gervase yesterday and brought them home because Annabel was ill. Then he drove me home here.'

'Why?'

Good question. 'My car wouldn't start so I had to get a taxi to Sophie's. I wasn't feeling great when it was time to leave so I accepted a lift home when James offered. He came round tonight to ask after Annabel.'

'I see.' He hesitated. 'You should take the day off tomorrow. I'll send Margaret to check on you in the morning. Now try to sleep. Goodnight.'

Harriet locked the door after him, then collected a couple of tonics from the fridge and went upstairs, groaning in relief when she finally slid into bed. The tonics were a godsend during her long, uncomfortable night. She woke with a start every time she fell into a doze, felt hot and cold in turns, ached all over, and felt deep sympathy for poor little Annabel. No wonder the child had just wanted to be cuddled. Not that Harriet had the least desire for any cuddling. She was just desperate for the sleep her headache wouldn't allow. At one stage she got up to take more painkillers, then banked the pillows behind her and just lay there to watch the sky grow light. When the office opened she rang Lydia to say she had a migraine and wouldn't be in that day.

Since it was almost unknown for Harriet to take a day off due to illness, Lydia sympathised warmly and told her to stay in bed until she was better. 'I'll inform the partners.'

Shortly afterwards Margaret arrived with a breakfast tray, and told Harriet to eat before she took any pills and then stay where she was until she felt better.

'Thank you, Margaret,' she said listlessly as a tray was laid across her knees. 'Sorry to add to your workload.'

'Nonsense,' said the woman briskly. 'Just you drink that tea while it's hot. Could you manage a poached egg?'

Harriet shuddered involuntarily. 'Tea and toast are just the ticket for now.'

'Is there anything else you want?'

'No, thanks.' Harriet smiled as she watched the neat, trim figure whisk out of the room, then rang Sophie to ask about Annabel, and heard the child was improving rapidly, but her sister was sure she was now coming down with the same virus.

'Please take a day off and come over again, Harriet. Gervase has to go into work today and I feel wretched.'

'Do you still have the nurse?'

'Yes, but she's just for Annabel. I need someone for me!'

'Sorry, Sophie. I'm in bed right now myself with a migraine. I feel wretched too.'

'*What?* But you're never ill!'

Harriet held her head as Margaret came in. 'Sophie,' she whispered, and Margaret promptly took the phone away from her.

'Margaret Rogers here. I'm afraid your sister's not well enough to keep talking right now, Sophie. She'll ring you back when she's up to it.' She listened for a while, then rolled her eyes at Harriet and said, 'What a shame. I hope you feel better soon.' She disconnected and handed the phone back.

'Thanks, Margaret,' said Harriet. 'Sophie wanted me to go over to her place to look after her.'

Margaret gave her a look that said plainly what she thought of that idea. 'I'll make you some fresh tea.'

Harriet left a message on the Old Rectory phone to postpone her lunch date with Moira for a couple of days, then gave herself up to the sleep her body craved. When she woke, to see Margaret tiptoeing in, it was early afternoon.

'Your father's downstairs. He wants to see you, Harriet. Are you up for that?'

Harriet blinked owlishly. 'I need a few minutes to tidy myself up.'

When Harriet was back in the bed Margaret had remade Aubrey tapped on the door, but stayed in the open doorway.

'How are you, Harriet?'

'My head has settled down a bit, but a migraine always leaves me feeling feeble for a bit.'

'You've obviously been overdoing things. You need a holiday.'

She frowned as the doorbell rang. 'Is Margaret down there?'

'No. She's out shopping. I'll see who it is.'

He came back a moment later with a vast basket of flowers. 'I've brought them up to show you, but then I'll take them downstairs in case they affect your head.'

Harriet stared at the extravagant display, her lips twitching as she read the message on the card.

Coals to Newcastle again. Get well soon. J.

'They're from James,' she informed her father.

His jaw clenched. 'I see. I'll take them down and leave you in peace, then. Margaret won't be long. Can I get you anything?'

'No, thanks.' She smiled a little. 'I'm drowsy again. It's all those pills.'

'By the way, I called in at the garage. The car's ready, and someone's driving it up here this afternoon.'

Next day Harriet had showered, dressed and graduated to the sofa downstairs to listen to an audio book, but was soon feeling so bored with her inactivity she was delighted when Moira Graveney arrived.

'If you don't feel up to it I can go away again, Harriet.'

'I'd love you to stay,' Harriet assured her.

Moira sat on the end of the sofa, eyeing Harriet closely. 'Are you better? Really? You don't look very marvellous.'

'Migraines tend to do that for me, but I'll be fine by tomorrow.'

'Has someone been taking care of you?'

'Margaret Rogers, the wonder woman who looks after River House. I need to get back on top form because Julia's bringing her crew down soon to do a photo shoot for her magazine,' said Harriet, pulling a face.

Moira laughed. 'Sounds like fun.' She looked at the basket of flowers in the window embrasure. 'Someone's been extravagant. Mr Corbett?'

'No. Your brother. Let's have some coffee,' said Harriet, getting up.

'I can make it,' said Moira promptly, but Harriet shook her head.

'I need to get back to normal.' She went off to the kitchen and came back with the drinks and a plate of almond biscuits. 'Margaret made these, too.'

'Tell her that if ever she wants to change jobs there's one waiting for her at the Old Rectory—these are heavenly.' Moira put her coffee down. 'Now, let's get to the reason for my visit. I did, of course, want to see how you are. But I also have a proposition to make.'

'Sounds exciting!'

'Marcus owns a cottage overlooking a tiny private beach in Pembrokeshire. You obviously need a break, so why not take time off and pop down there for a couple of days? It would do you good to just lie in the sun, if there is any, and eat dinner in the local pub. What do you say?'

Harriet eyed her, tempted. 'It sounds like an offer I can't refuse.'

'Then don't. I think you'd like it there. Take some food basics with you, but there's a very good village store.' Moira smiled. 'And the cottage will be immaculate, because Mrs Pugh who cleans it for us believes that cleanliness is next to Godliness, and in that order. So what do you say?' She took out a key and dangled it in front of Harriet's eyes.

Why not do something impulsive for once? Harriet smiled warmly. 'I say yes, Mrs Graveney. Thank you very much indeed.' She thought for a moment. 'I'll go down tomorrow, if that's all right with you.'

'Absolutely fine. Let's hope nothing crops up in your life to get in the way. How's your little niece doing?'

'Much improved once Gervase hired a paediatric nurse to take care of her. But the real boost to Annabel's recovery was the news that the Spanish girl who normally looks after her is returning to the Barclay household soon. It was a boost for my sister, too. Sophie was sure she was coming down with the same virus, but when she heard about Pilar she made a miraculous recovery.'

'James told me he met your sister at some lunch party, while you were looking after her daughter, and then drove you home afterwards because you looked so exhausted.'

'It was very kind of him.'

'He says your sister looks nothing at all like you.'

'No. She's the pretty one. Julia is the brilliant one, and I'm—'

'The hardworking one everyone relies on from the way your father talked about you at the party,' said Moira, and grinned. 'Though that was a bit hard to swallow when you wowed us with your tango!'

Harriet grinned back. 'I get a mad moment now and then like anyone else, so I'll have one now and snatch that key from you to skive off to Wales.'

'That's the spirit!'

Harriet paused, thinking—as she did far too much— of the dream-like episode in her bedroom. Had she really kissed James or had she just wanted to? Either way, she didn't fancy talking to him any time soon. 'Would you do me a favour? Could you pass on my thanks to James for the flowers? Tell him they were much appreciated.'

After Moira left Harriet's recovery was rapid at the prospect of a weekend away from River House which, much as she loved it, sometimes felt like a millstone weighing her down. Her mood was boosted even further when her father called in with a parcel containing a paperback crime novel and the DVD of a film she'd been looking forward to seeing. The note with it said:

I heard you were off sick, and thought the enclosed would appeal. Love, Nick.

'How very nice of him,' Harriet exclaimed.

'I mentioned you were under the weather when I was in the bank today so he asked me to call back after lunch for this,' said Aubrey. 'You look better now. Mrs Graveney obviously cheered you up.'

Harriet told him about her proposed trip at the weekend, rather surprised to find her father strongly approved.

'Splendid idea—do you the world of good. Let's hope for good weather. You'll need to be fit for Julia's fashion shoot, so take a break while you can.'

'Have you found somewhere to stay during the shoot?'

'Oh, yes, no problem there,' he assured her, but didn't give details and Harriet didn't ask for any.

Harriet was thoughtful after he'd gone. It had been a surprise to learn that her father thought of her with any approval at all, let alone as the most reliable of his three daughters. The mad moments she hadn't told Moira about were few, but, unlike the tango, some had resulted in life-altering developments. The first had been her plan to leave home to live with James Crawford. When her father put a stop to that her eventual demand to take over the Lodge permanently had struck the final blow to détente between them. Yet lately, once he'd recovered from his anger over her deception about James and the party, Aubrey Wilde had been in a more conciliatory mood than usual, which made her suspicious. If he imagined she might return to live with him at River House he was sadly mistaken.

CHAPTER ELEVEN

MOIRA GRAVENEY rang her brother that night, at a late enough hour to put him on the alert.

'Something wrong, love?' he asked.

'Afraid so, but I don't know exactly what, yet. Marcus had to rush off to London tonight to deal with a family crisis. He'll ring me later, when he finds out what's wrong.'

'Claudia, as usual?'

'No, it's Lily for once. Marcus wasn't given details; her mother just requested some immediate family support, and as this is pretty rare he took off right away.'

'Try not to worry—and let me know when you have more news.'

'I'll ring you tomorrow. By the way, I drove round to see Harriet today.'

'How is she?'

'She's better. Still a bit fragile, but the migraine had just about gone. She asked me to pass on a message of thanks for your flowers, by the way.'

James's lips tightened. Couldn't she have rung him herself?

'Did you hear what I said?' demanded Moira.

'Harriet said thanks for the flowers,' he repeated bleakly.

'No, the next bit,' she said impatiently. 'I suggested she

could do with a break and gave her the key to the cottage. She's driving down there tomorrow for the weekend.'

His eyes narrowed. 'You do surprise me. If by some miracle Harriet took time off from her beloved work I thought she'd be back at her sister's, looking after her niece.'

'A paediatric nurse has been hired for that. Though, reading between the lines, it's obvious that Harriet is the go-to girl for any emergency in the Wilde family.'

'But she's actually going to please herself for once. Amazing.'

'Don't be cynical, James. I don't know what happened between you two in the past, but I like Harriet very much.'

You're not the only one, thought James bitterly as he closed his phone. Though 'like' seemed hardly the right word. Whatever he had once felt for Harriet Wilde was still alive and well, even though she'd once broken his life in pieces by dumping him. And soon, he promised himself grimly, he would find out exactly what had made her do it.

Harriet was packed and ready the next day for her getaway when her father, rather to her surprise, came to load her bags into the car along with a box of supplies Margaret had put together. He hesitated as she got in the car, and then patted her hand. 'Come back with some colour in your cheeks. Have you packed medication in case your headache comes back?'

Harriet assured him that she had, and drove off feeling like a child let out of school as she waved him goodbye.

The day was cool and cloudy for the majority of the journey, but after she left the motorway at Carmarthen the sun came out in such blinding glory she snapped her visor down and donned dark glasses. West Wales was giving her a warm welcome. After negotiating the steep market town of Haverfordwest, Harriet headed towards the sun and eventually turned down a narrow winding road which gave exciting glimpses of sea at every hairpin bend and brought her at last to a small foursquare house sitting on a ledge carved out of the cliff, with a steep path leading from it to the private cove below. She backed into the small parking area beside the house, then got out of the car, shading her eyes to look with pleasure at the panorama below. She unlocked the door in the small porch and after a quick survey of the small kitchen took everything from the car and virtuously put the food away before taking a trip down to the beach. At last she crammed a sunhat on her head, put the house key in her pocket and went exploring.

Harriet hurried down the steep path past tufts of grass and sea drift which brushed against her jeans as the siren song of breaking waves lured her down at speed to the crescent of pebbles edging the sand. Breathless after her headlong descent, she drew in a deep breath of pure delight at the sight of sunlight reflected on rippling waves. Her previous holidays by the sea had been very different from this secluded Welsh cove. When the Wilde girls were small, holidays had been spent in Torquay or Bournemouth, in the large comfortable hotels her parents had preferred. And after the trauma with James she'd done some determined partying with student friends in Ibiza.

After a while her rumbling stomach reminded her that she was hungry, and Harriet went back up to explore the rest of the house before making herself some lunch. Comfortable furniture and cheerful chintz suited the character of the solid old cottage, and the small guest room had an inviting brass bed and a deep window embrasure with a view of the beach.

Unpacking done, Harriet went down the steep stairs later looking forward to a meal for the first time in ages.

She made a salad to eat with Margaret's roast ham and enjoyed it at a small table in the sitting room window. With a concert on the radio for background and a view of the beach to look at, for the first time in what seemed forever Harriet began to feel relaxed. She left a message on her father's phone to say she'd arrived, and then went down to the beach to take advantage of the sunshine. Later on, after she'd showered and dressed, she thought about going out for supper at the pub Moira had recommended, but by that time she was feeling the effects of her journey and opted for a lazy evening in front of the television.

Harriet slept better that night than she'd done in weeks. She woke early to the raucous cries of seagulls and ran to the window to check on the weather, delighted to find sunshine again. After breakfast she rang for news of Annabel and was told that she was improving rapidly, but Sophie couldn't see why Harriet had driven all the way to West Wales for a break when she could have come back to Pennington. Harriet promised to do so soon, sent her love to Annabel, and then rang Moira.

'I arrived safely, the sun is shining, and this is such a charming cottage, Moira. I can't thank you enough for letting me stay here.'

'You're very welcome. Get out in that sunshine and enjoy yourself. It's good to hear that someone's happy.'

Was something wrong with James? 'You sound a bit down, Moira.'

'I am. Marcus had to take off to London to sort out a family problem and came back with a desperately unhappy Lily.'

'Oh, poor Lily. I don't want to pry, but do you know what's wrong?'

'She won't say, exactly. Marcus is at his wit's end, poor darling. He's unmoved by Claudia's dramas, but Lily's tears are cutting him to pieces. As far as we can tell, it's to do with Dominic, so we'll just give her support and sympathy until she tells us what we can do to help. But that's enough of my woes—I want you to enjoy your holiday.'

'I will. I'll ring you when I get back.'

Harriet put her phone on charge, and then drove off to stock up at the village stores before she went on with her sea, sun and sand programme. By the time she got back the sun was hot. She changed into a bikini, slathered herself with sunscreen and took a packed tote bag down to the beach to sunbathe.

Hunger, plus respect for the sun, drove Harriet back up to the house after only a short spell of sunbathing. After lunch, mindful that she was here for a rest, she lay propped up on her bed with the window open to the sea breezes while she left a message on Julia's phone in case her sister needed to be in touch over the forthcoming photo shoot. Duty done, Harriet put her phone with the rest of her belongings and went down to the beach again. She found a new spot to take advantage of the hot afternoon sun, but when sunbathing palled after a while she went for a swim. She waded until she could dive into the waves and struck out with a workmanlike crawl across the small cove. On the way back she coughed, swallowed a mouthful of water and sputtered irritably, wishing she'd kept to paddling. And screamed her head off when a hard arm came round her chest and an inexorable hand held her chin up as her rescuer began to tow her back to shore.

'Quiet! Keep still, for God's sake,' grated a breathless, furious voice as her legs kicked out. 'You're out of danger, so relax and let me do the work.'

When her panting rescuer finally stood up in the shallows, Harriet slid to her feet and backed away, glaring at him without gratitude.

'What the blazes are *you* doing here, James Crawford?' she panted, the breath whistling through her chest.

Good question, he thought grimly. Behaving like an utter fool by the look of it.

'I was enjoying a peaceful swim out there until you arrived,' she informed him.

Breathing hard, James thrust a hand through his streaming hair. 'Peaceful!' He took her by the shoulders and shook her slightly. 'I thought you were drowning, woman. There's a hell of an undertow here further out. I thought you were caught in it.'

'I wasn't idiot enough to go out that far! The only danger was cardiac arrest when you grabbed me!' Harriet hurried across the sand, coughing up water as she bent to pick up her towel.

James eyed her grimly as he gathered up the sweater and shoes he'd discarded. His wet jeans moulded every muscular inch of him so faithfully that after one look Harriet buried her hot face in the towel. 'It's stupidity to swim here alone.'

Harriet ground her teeth, anger boiling about in a stew of several other emotions. She took in a few careful breaths, and emerged from her towel to face him. 'You'd better come up to the cottage to get dry.' She tugged on her espadrilles and climbed up to the house, leaving James to follow behind on bare wet feet, cursing at loose pebbles as he went.

James took a suitcase from the boot of his car as she unlocked the door.

'Don't worry; I just want some dry clothes,' he said, smiling sardonically at the look she threw at him. 'I'm booked in at the hotel on the Point.'

'You're on holiday here?' Harriet said incredulously, and took two towels from the rack by the sink. She handed him one and used the other to rub vainly at the salty wet tangle of her hair. 'Not that it matters. I won't be staying long. I'm sure we can keep out of each other's hair until I leave.'

'That's a cold reception for a man who's just driven all the way across England and Wales in time to save you from drowning,' he retorted.

'I was not *drowning*,' she said through her teeth. 'Does Moira know you're here?'

'I told her I might call in while I was in the area.' He looked at her steadily. 'But if you object to my presence I'll take myself off.'

She shook her head. 'I don't object, James. Have you eaten?'

'No. I came here first before checking in. Which is a damn good thing. It took years off my life when I saw you flailing about in the sea.'

'I was not flailing,' she said, dangerously quiet. 'And now we both need to get dry—'

'You first,' he said instantly. 'Get in a really hot shower. I'll have one after you, and then I'll take you out to dinner.'

'Yes to the shower, no to dinner,' she said flatly, and took off up the stairs, leaving him scowling after her.

Instead of the bath she longed for, Harriet stood under blessedly hot water in the shower for a short time, then pulled on her hooded towelling robe and went to the head of the stairs. 'All yours,' she yelled, and shut herself in her bedroom to work on her hair. When she finally emerged in jeans and white shirt, her damp curls tied up on top of her head, the bathroom was empty. Bracing herself for another confrontation, she went down to the sitting room.

James looked at her in silence for a moment. Dressed like that, without a scrap of make-up, she looked so much like the girl he'd once been crazy about he felt a sudden urge to tear her clothes off. With his teeth. He took in a deep, unsteady breath and waved a hand at his own choice of clothes. 'Snap!'

Harriet forced a smile. The man had driven a long way. His life-saving act had been annoying and unnecessary but the fact remained that he'd charged straight into the sea to her rescue. 'I've got some wine, if you'd care for a drink, or I could make you some tea. I need something to warm me up.'

'I'm not surprised. That sea may look beautiful in the sun, but it's really cold when you get in it! Tea would be good, Harriet. Then I'll take you out for a meal.' He ran his eyes over her. 'You look as though you could do with one.'

'I don't want to go out.'

His grin vanished. 'You mean not with me.'

'I mean I'm a bit tired after all the drama,' she said impatiently.

Her tone killed his sudden blaze of lust stone dead. 'Don't bother about the tea,' James said crisply. 'I'll take myself off and go alone in search of dinner.'

'I *meant* I can cook for us here—if you like.'

'You said you were tired,' he pointed out.

'Not too tired to cook something simple. Give me twenty minutes or so and I'll have a meal on the table,' said Harriet. After all he had come a long way.

'Then I accept. Give me something to do.'

It felt odd to be scrubbing potatoes while James shelled broad beans, so much so that when he'd finished Harriet suggested he caught up with the television news in the other room while she got on with the meal. To offset the illicit feeling of intimacy, she busied herself with laying the table, cutting bread and hulling strawberries, then snipped rashers of locally cured bacon and put them under the grill.

James joined her, sniffing hungrily. 'Something smells good.'

Harriet served the food straight on to warm plates and took them into the sitting room. 'How are things with Live Wires?' she asked politely as James drew out a chair for her.

'Going from strength to strength now the new companies are incorporated.' He sat down, eyeing the food in anticipation. 'This looks delicious. I eat so much fancy stuff at dinners a simple meal like this is a treat.'

'First of the Pembroke new potatoes, broad beans picked this morning, and locally reared bacon, all from the village shop up on the main road,' she informed him.

There was silence between them as they enjoyed the food. When James pushed his empty plate away he sat back, watching Harriet finish her meal. 'I've never told Moira,' he said abruptly.

She looked up, startled. 'Told her what, exactly? She knows we once knew each other.'

'But not that you were the one who murdered my boyish illusions,' he said, taking her breath away. 'Not that I'm ungrateful; far from it. Your rejection spurred me on to make a success of my life.'

Harriet put her half full plate on top of his empty one and got up. 'Would you like some strawberries?' she said steadily.

He shook his head in sardonic wonder. 'I bare my soul and all you can talk about is strawberries?'

'I can't rewrite the past, James. Obviously hiring River House wasn't enough revenge for this soul of yours.' Her eyes narrowed. 'Did you come all this way just to heap more recriminations on my head?'

He jumped up, towering over her angrily. 'No. I came here to enjoy your company for a while in neutral surroundings, so we can talk like two civilised people. But obviously I've been a bloody fool. Again.'

Harriet took the plates into the kitchen, and ran water into the sink and shut the door behind her so he wouldn't hear her as she coughed up more salt water. Sheer iron will had prevented her from giving into it while he was shouting at her, but now the cough defeated her and she leaned over the sink, gasping helplessly after it was over. The door flew open and James filled a glass with water and held it to her mouth. Her mouth twisted. She really had to stop leaning over kitchen sinks with James.

'Thank you,' she managed at last, and drank the water.

He took the glass from her, refilled it and turned off the tap, and then led her out of the kitchen into the sitting room. He put the glass on a small table alongside the sofa and told her to sit down. 'Have you recovered completely from your migraine?'

'Yes.'

'Do you get them often?'

'No, but when I do they're so bad I hardly know what I'm doing.'

'I noticed.'

She glared at him. 'What, exactly, do you mean by that?'

'Your usual iron control was missing the other night. Otherwise, I doubt you'd have let me put you to bed. What if a migraine strikes again while you're here on your own?' he said, frowning.

Harriet drank some water. 'It won't. Last time it was caused by an unusual combination of circumstances. I'd had a very worrying time with Annabel, hadn't managed to eat all day—'

'And to add to your joys I shocked the hell out of you by turning up at your sister's house,' he said grimly.

'I wouldn't have put it quite like that.'

'Can you deny that the sight of me added to your stress factor?'

'No. Though I was grateful for the lift home. Then I had meetings with clients all next day, one of which required a long drive in an unfamiliar car.' Harriet looked at him squarely. 'Enough of my problems. Tell me the truth, James. Why are you here?'

His eyes lit with a gleam, which made her deeply uneasy. 'It seemed too good an opportunity to pass up when Moira told me you were coming here. I was sure that if we spent enough uninterrupted time together you would tell me the truth at last.' His mouth compressed. 'For years I thought I didn't care a damn about it any more. Then I met you again and found it was vital to learn what turned you from a warm, loving girl into the wary professional woman I found in that office.'

She eyed him in silence for a moment, then shrugged. 'Life changed me, James, just as it changed you from the loving carefree man you used to be. So can't we just call it quits? I'm sorry for the way it ended between us all those years ago, but I can't keep on apologising, James. It's time to move on.' She paused, then when he made no response, shrugged, defeated. 'If you feel you came all this way for nothing I'm sorry you're disappointed, but now I suggest you drive to your hotel and let me get to bed.'

James went on eyeing her in unsettling silence for a while, and then shook his head. 'I don't want to leave you alone here like this, Harriet. You go up to bed. I'll stay here on the sofa.'

She glared at him. 'Don't be ridiculous. Neither of us would sleep.'

'Possibly not, but at least I'd be here at hand if you needed me.'

'Why should I need you? I'm absolutely fine.' She closed her eyes in frustration. 'James. Please. Just go.'

He shrugged. 'If that's what you want I will eventually, but not yet. Now I've come all this way, we can at least talk for a while. I'll make you some tea, or whatever.'

'Oh, very well,' she said, resigned. 'But I'd better do that.'

'No need,' he assured her. 'I know where things are because Marcus gives me carte blanche to come here on my own whenever I need to get away, which isn't often lately. When I'm not up to my ears in it at work I'm overseeing progress with my house. I won't be long.'

Harriet leaned back, trying to relax, but it was hard with James on hand. Her wildest dreams hadn't come up with this scenario for her holiday. She'd just wanted to enjoy her unexpected break, and get herself back to full strength to deal with whatever life had in store over the next few months. One thing she was sure of. Once the finances of River House were on an even keel again her father could take full responsibility for the house. Julia was right. Their mother would not have wanted her to devote her entire life to it.

James came back with a tray and set it down beside her. 'You used to like your tea strong with a dash of milk,' he said, handing her a mug.

'I still do. Thank you.' Harriet smiled, secretly touched that he remembered.

'I opted for coffee to keep me awake on the drive to the hotel.' He looked at her in silence for a moment. 'In jeans, and with your hair like that, you look very young tonight, Harriet.'

'I'm twenty-nine, not Methuselah!' she retorted, and he laughed.

'I know exactly how old you are. By the way, did you

think it was pure altruism that brought me to your sister's house last Sunday?'

Harriet stared. 'It wasn't?'

He shook his head. 'It's true that I gave your sister and her husband a lift when they were in a hurry to get home to their child. But I had been talking to Sophie on and off right through the lunch, and she was very forthcoming with her personal details. I learned that she was not only your sister, but that you were looking after her daughter.' His eyes held hers. 'I jumped at the offer when they invited me in for a drink when we arrived. But you were too taken up with your little niece to pay attention to me, or anyone else. Is she better now?'

'Yes, she is.' Harriet eyed him blankly. 'Are you saying you drove Sophie and Gervase back just to see me?'

'I like to think I would have done so anyway in the circumstances, but the prospect of seeing you was my main motivation. Is that so hard to believe?'

'Yes. I thought you still felt hostile towards me.'

'I did once.' James shrugged. 'But I won't pretend I spent all those years thinking of ways to get back at you, or even thinking of you at all in time.'

Harriet felt a sharp pang of pain. Of course he'd stopped thinking of her. She'd stopped thinking of him every minute of the day in time, too. Some days, anyway.

'In fact,' continued James, 'until Marcus bought the Old Rectory in your neck of the woods, I'd been too busy building up Live Wires into a successful venture to have much time for regrets about the past.'

'It must have felt like your lucky day finding out River House was for hire!'

'It was certainly the perfect cure for the festering hurt I'd kept locked away at the back of my mind all those years.' His smile set her teeth on edge.

'So now you're satisfied.' Harriet shrugged. 'But it rather backfired on you, James, because I'm satisfied too.'

James looked at her in silence for so long Harriet was beginning to fidget by the time he spoke again. 'So come clean at last—tell me what really happened all those years ago,' he ordered, startling her. 'One minute you were as happy as a lark about renting a house together, the next minute I was being relocated from my job and you were giving me my marching orders. I was so furious it was only later, when the red mist cleared from my brain, that I realised you were as miserable as hell that day too. Tell me the truth, Harriet. Your father didn't approve of our plan, did he?'

'No, he didn't.'

'And you weren't brave enough to defy him and take off with me.'

'No, I wasn't.'

'Your father's pretty hostile towards me now he's found out who I am.'

'Hardly surprising! He went up like a rocket when George Lassiter gave him the glad news. Father assumed that you and I were laughing together behind his back the night of the party until I told him you still felt hostile towards me. Which you do,' she added.

James's smile raised the short curling hairs on the back of her neck. 'Harriet, what I'm feeling right now has nothing to do with hostility.' He moved nearer. 'You owe me.'

She backed away. 'For what, exactly?'

'I saved your life this afternoon.' The look in his eyes rang Harriet's alarm bells.

'Except that my life was in no danger,' she retorted and got up, but he tugged on her hand and pulled her down on his lap.

'It's the thought that counts, so I deserve at least one

kiss,' he said huskily, in the tone that had turned her to jelly when she was a teenager.

Harriet wondered if he could hear her heart hammering in her chest, and put on a martyred expression as she held up her mouth. 'Oh, all right.'

James's laugh set the alarm bells ringing even louder as he pulled her closer. 'You look as though you're making the supreme sacrifice. Is the thought of kissing me so repugnant, Harriet?'

'No—' She gasped as his mouth came down on hers with a kiss she felt right down to her toes. His arms tightened around her in a possession she surrendered to helplessly, her lips opening to his caressing tongue as he made love to her in the way which had left her crying into her pillow for too many nights all those years ago. And now it was happening again. The mere touch of his lips set her on fire, but when his urgent fingers went to work on her shirt buttons Harriet pushed him away.

'More payback?' she demanded raggedly. She struggled to get up, but he kept his arms around her, holding her fast until she gave up struggling and lay quiet against him.

'I'm taking you to bed,' he said in a tone which quelled all argument. Not that Harriet was about to argue. Bed with James at last would solve a lot of her problems. She stopped thinking as he kissed her with a heat that blotted out everything other than the joy of being held fast against his chest, feeling his heart thudding against hers.

'I want this a damn sight more than any revenge,' he muttered against her mouth.

'Come to bed, then,' she said recklessly.

His smile turned her heart over. 'I've waited ten long years to hear you say that. Up you come.' He swung her up in his arms and made for the stairs. 'Next time you walk up. Tonight I'll do my Rhett Butler act.'

'Lovely.' Harriet smiled up at him in such invitation he kissed her fiercely as he took off her jeans and shirt, then laid her on the bed and threw off his clothes to slide in beside her. His eyes moved over her in slow, hot relish for a while before he ran a hand over her lacy tank and briefs. 'These are pretty. Take them off.'

'You want them off, you take them off,' she responded, surprising herself and James by the way he laughed unsteadily before following orders.

'At last,' he breathed, as they came together skin to skin. 'I never dared undress you all those years ago because you were so determined to wait until we lived together before sharing a bed. While I wanted to get you into mine the moment I first set eyes on you.'

'Let's not talk of years ago. This is now, James. Make love to me at last,' she begged.

'I will,' he whispered, and kissed her mouth for a long, breathless interval, before going on to kiss every bare inch of her he could reach, some of which took her so much by surprise she moaned and shivered in the throes of guilty solo pleasure before James slid over her and inside her to take her with him on a wild, uninhibited climb to the orgasm he reached first and stayed locked within her until she gasped against him in the throes of her own delight.

Expecting him to roll away, Harriet was utterly ravished when James held her tightly afterwards as though he couldn't bear to let her go, and eventually, to her utter astonishment, she felt him harden again inside her as he turned her mouth up to his to kiss her and make love to her all over again, but more slowly the second time, with such tenderness she cried when it was over and he licked away her tears and smoothed the wild tangle of curls away from her forehead.

'Are you crying for joy because I'm so good at this?' he

asked smugly, and Harriet gave a gurgle of laughter as he rolled away, taking her with him to hold her in the crook of his arm.

'Such hubris!' She raised her head to look at him. 'How about the hotel?'

'I lied about booking there,' he said, grinning shamelessly.

'What if I'd shown you the door and hadn't let you stay?' she asked curiously.

'Plan A was battering the door until you gave in, the less popular plan B was sleeping in the car.' James threaded his fingers through her unruly curls. 'But you didn't make me go. Why?'

'Because I was nervous here on my own.'

'Of course you were.' He tucked her head into his shoulder. 'Now go to sleep.'

When Harriet woke up it was morning. She turned her head cautiously and met a pair of eyes gleaming like gold coins in the early sunlight.

'Hello,' said James softly.

'Good morning.' Harriet smiled and tried to sit up but a hard arm restrained her.

'Not yet.' He drew her close, the hunger of his kiss setting her on fire for him again as they united in the hot, earthy joy of wake up love. They were quiet in each other's arms for a while afterwards, drowsy with content until he raised her face to his. 'Now I have you at my mercy it's confession time, Harriet. Tell me the truth at last. I know your father disapproved, but the girl I knew wanted to be with me too much to let that break us up. So talk. Tell me what happened to change your mind all those years ago.'

She sat up, smiling bitterly. 'Oh, I *see*. All this was Plan C, James Crawford!' She stabbed a hand at the untidy bed.

'Literally hands-on persuasion to get the truth out of me at last.' She leapt from the bed to wrap herself in her dressing gown, utterly mortified that she'd been fool enough to believe he was desperate to make love to her, while all the time it was his way of slotting the last piece of the jigsaw into place.

James pulled on his jeans and stalked towards her, a look in his eyes she disliked intensely. 'Just to set the record straight, Harriet, there was no persuasion involved. Was there?'

Burning colour flooded her face as she made for the bathroom and locked the door behind her. She brushed her teeth and washed her face with a violence that made it even redder, and took as long as she could over the process. At last she unlocked the door, brushed past James on the landing and went into the bedroom to dress before hurrying downstairs. When James joined her in the kitchen she gave him no chance to speak.

'I'd like you to leave now, please.'

He shook his head, eyes hard. 'Not before you tell me the truth at last.'

For a moment Harriet was tempted. After all, did it really matter so much any more? And if it caused trouble between James Crawford and her father did she care? What a fool she'd been. Making love with James at long last had been the rapture she'd always known it would be, but for him it had merely been the most effective form of persuasion.

'You exerted your considerable sexual talent just for that?' she said without emotion. 'Or was getting me into bed at long last the final touch to your payback programme?'

James's eyes blazed with cold distaste. 'No, it was not. And if that's how your mind works these days it doesn't matter a damn why you sent me packing back then—I'm just grateful you did.' He strode to the door but closed it softly behind him in a far bigger statement than slamming it shut.

Sheer pride made Harriet stay on at the cottage until the Monday. The weather, at least, was perfect. She was able to sunbathe all she wanted, but no matter how high the temperature rose she couldn't face the thought of swimming. She ate sensibly and went for regular walks each day. She even went as far as the village shop, and found the exercise energised her. She was pleased with herself. She was no maiden falling into a decline over a man. She'd been there, done that once already over the same man. But last time she'd been in the depths of despair because she'd been forced to hurt James. This time the shoe was on the other foot, and God, how it hurt!

Her phone kept her from feeling lonely. Moira rang to report that Dominic had come to see Lily, and she'd allowed him to stay the night. Aubrey Wilde rang to ask when she was coming back, so did Miriam, and Julia called with a reminder about the photo shoot. Charlotte Brewster contacted Harriet to confirm dates for the TV filming sessions in River House, and the cookery shot on schedule later, and said the bed retailers wanted to repaint the veranda bedroom in their trademark shade of pomegranate. Since Charlotte had negotiated a higher fee for this Harriet was all for it. She got in touch with Lydia and asked her to inform the partners that she would be back on Tuesday to meet with two of her clients on schedule, then rang to ask after Annabel, and learned that both Sophie and her daughter were in tearing spirits because Pilar was arriving next day. From James there was only silence.

The day before she left Cliff Cottage Harriet cleaned

every inch of it to make sure Mrs Pugh would have no complaints after she departed, and reported her hard work when Moira rang with the news that Lily had gone back to London with Dominic.

'Did you find out what was wrong?'

'The poor darling thought she was pregnant, but it was a false alarm.'

'Why wouldn't she tell her mother?'

'Who knows? She only told me about it once she knew she wasn't. Dominic promptly asked, and received, Marcus's permission to marry Lily, and produced a ring on the spot, so all's well that ends well.' Moira sighed. 'I'm glad I only had brothers! Talking of which, James bit my head off when I asked him how you were enjoying your break at the cottage.' She hesitated. 'Did you two have some kind of disagreement?'

'Good heavens, no,' lied Harriet brightly, and began discussing possible dates with Moira for the lunch they'd postponed.

Harriet woke up early on the Monday morning to rain, which suited her mood as she ate some breakfast. Afterwards, she transferred her belongings to the car and locked the house carefully behind her, took a last look at the view, then slid behind the wheel and turned on the ignition. Nothing happened. With a groan of pure frustration she tried again, and then again, and at last, cursing the mechanic at home who was supposed to have put the car right only a few days ago, rang the garage attached to the village stores. To her infinite gratitude she was promised help right away, and within minutes a pickup arrived with a cheery young man who put his head under the bonnet of her car and soon diagnosed the problem.

'It's the starter motor. You'll need a new one, miss, but

I'll have to send off for one, which would take a couple of days.'

She smiled at him ruefully. 'Then can I leave it with you? I'll come back at the weekend to collect it. In the meantime, can you give me some information about trains? I must get home today.'

With a cheery efficiency Harriet deeply appreciated, the mechanic, who introduced himself as Evan Johns, son of the proprietor of both stores and garage, gave her the times of trains from Haverfordwest, and even offered to drive her there.

'This is so kind of you,' said Harriet when they were on their way.

'No problem. I can catch up with my list when I get back—I rang my dad to explain.'

Harriet was on the station platform in Haverfordwest, waiting for her train when Moira rang.

'Sorry to keep hassling you, Harriet, but if you haven't started out yet could you bring the Michael Connelly novel Marcus left behind last time?'

When Harriet explained why she wouldn't be able to do that Moira sympathised and insisted on picking her up from the train in Shrewsbury.

'I can't let you do that! I'll get a taxi.'

'Certainly not; it would cost a fortune. It's a pleasant drive and now all the excitement's over my time is my own, so I'll be there, waiting for you.'

But to Harriet's consternation it was James, in formal city suit, who met her from the train.

'My sister sends her apologies but there's an emergency with the Old Rectory plumbing and Marcus is in court today,' he informed her, taking her bags.

'She shouldn't have asked *you* to come for me,' said Harriet, dismayed. 'I told her I could take a taxi.'

'I had business in the area,' he said coldly. 'It's not a problem.'

Not for him, maybe, but a car journey alone with James Crawford in the present circumstances was the last thing Harriet wanted. 'It's very kind of you,' she said tightly as he stowed her luggage.

'Not at all.' He shot a glance at her as he tossed his jacket on the back seat. 'How are you?'

'Very well, thank you.'

'Did you do any more swimming?'

'No.'

'Very sensible.'

Silence fell. Harriet, grateful for dark glasses, stared through the windscreen, and though not normally a speed fan, willed him to drive faster to get this over with.

'You heard about Lily?' James asked after a while.

'Yes.'

He shot a searching glance at her. 'It struck me that there could be similar worries for you after our night together.'

Harriet's stomach gave a sickening lurch. 'There won't,' she said baldly, and fervently hoped she was right. Her one fleeting experience of contraceptive pills in college had been so unpleasant she had never taken them again.

'Good,' he said, equally terse.

Harriet endured the rest of the endless journey in silence. It felt like hours before James finally turned up the River House drive to the Lodge.

'Thank you so much.' She smiled coolly as he took her bags from the car. 'I'm sure you're in a hurry to be off so I won't ask you to come in.'

'Don't be stupid,' he said impatiently. 'Having collected you from the blasted train, I can spare a moment to carry your luggage inside.'

Stony-faced, Harriet unlocked the door and went inside,

dismayed to find that the Lodge sitting room felt small and claustrophobic after the not much bigger Cliff Cottage. How stupid was that? But then she was stupid, according to James. 'Thank you,' she said brusquely as he stood holding the bags.

'I'll just take these upstairs for you—'

'*No,*' said Harriet involuntarily. 'I'll unpack them down here. Easier for laundry.'

He put them down. 'In that case I'll take myself off.'

'Goodbye, and thank you again for the lift.'

He looked down at her, his face grim. 'Before I go, let's get something clear. I was brought up to honour my obligations, so if you find you are expecting my child, I'll do the right thing.'

Harriet stared at him, speechless for a moment. 'How very noble of you,' she said at last. 'But even if something so unlikely should happen, the right thing won't be necessary.'

His eyes glittered with such cold ferocity she had to fight to stand her ground. 'Because I'm still not socially acceptable for Miss Wilde of River House?'

Harriet suddenly lost her temper. 'Oh for God's sake, get rid of the chip on your shoulder, James Crawford. I meant that in the unlikely event that I marry anyone, ever, it won't be someone forced into it to "do the right thing".'

'Who mentioned marriage?' he snarled and strode out of the house to gun the Aston Martin down the drive to the road.

CHAPTER TWELVE

ENRAGED by James's parting shot, Harriet was too furious to walk up to the house to report in. Her father was probably out, anyway, and Margaret would have finished for the day long since. But a look in the kitchen confirmed that before leaving Margaret had stocked Harriet's fridge and bread bin. For some reason this was the last straw. Harriet laid her head on her arms on the counter and gave way to a flood of bitter tears which, far from giving relief, only made her feel worse when they finally stopped. She splashed her face with cold water, then fetched her bags and decanted most of her laundry straight into the washing machine. The new nightwear James had taken off in such a hurry was thrust in a plastic bag and binned.

Harriet had a quick shower, did her face and hair, and checked the garage. When she saw her father's car there she went into the house via the back door.

'Hello,' she called as she went inside. 'Anybody home?'

Aubrey Wilde came hurrying into the kitchen, smartly dressed as usual. 'Harriet! You look really well. You obviously enjoyed your little holiday.'

'I did, very much. I thought I'd just report in before I eat.'

'Good, good. Come along to the drawing room. Now you're here, there's someone I'd like you to meet.'

Antennae quivering when her father took her hand to enter the drawing room, Harriet smiled politely at the woman who rose from the sofa at their entry. She was tall, with a slim athletic figure and expensively cut ash-blonde hair framing a handsome suntanned face. 'Harriet,' said her father, 'I'd like you to meet Madeleine Fox.'

Mrs Fox! Harriet freed her hand to hold it out. 'How do you do?'

Madeleine took the hand in a strong grip and shook it briefly. 'It's good to meet you at last. Aubrey's told me so much about you.'

Surprise news to Harriet. 'Do you live locally?'

'I moved into Fossedyke Court a few months ago.' Madeleine smiled. 'I still feel like the new kid on the block here, but Aubrey's been very kind in making me feel welcome at the golf club.'

'She plays off eight,' Aubrey told Harriet with pride.

'Quite a compliment from a scratch player,' Madeleine returned, smiling at him, and turned to Harriet. 'You have a beautiful home.'

Praise indeed from someone who lived in a Jacobean manor house. 'It's lovely,' agreed Harriet, 'but quite a responsibility.'

'So is mine. But I've inherited it so I've just got to get on with it. My boys would prefer me to live in something more modern and easy, but they both work in London, so I rattle around there on my own.'

No Mr Fox, then.

'When exactly is Julia coming down, Harriet?' asked Aubrey.

'On Sunday, ready for the shoot on Monday. Have you organised somewhere to stay?'

'Madeleine's offered to put me up.' He flushed slightly. 'But that's on Monday. I thought we'd get Sophie over so we can all have dinner together on Sunday. I've spoken to Margaret and she'll do the meal.'

'Aubrey says you've been to West Wales. You obviously had good weather,' said Madeleine.

'I was lucky with that. It was good to have a break, but I get back to work tomorrow.' Harriet looked at her father. 'Do you want me to get in touch with Sophie about the meal?'

'No, dear, I already have.'

'I'll say goodnight, then.'

'Good to meet you, Harriet,' said Madeleine Fox. 'See you on Sunday.'

So Mrs Fox was joining the party. Harriet went back to the Lodge in a thoughtful mood. Her father had been a widower for a long time, but, as far as she knew, had never brought a woman here before. Margaret would have known if he had. If he'd had liaisons, which a man like him must have done, they'd been conducted somewhere else. Madeleine Fox was the first woman to dine at River House. Did that mean her father would like her to move into it with him? If so, it would be the end of Harriet's sojourn at the Lodge. She would find somewhere in town.

After a quick word with Moira, who apologised for failing to meet her at Shrewsbury, Harriet kept the peace by ringing Miriam to say she was back, then finally ate some soup and went early to bed, if not early to sleep. Not that she had expected to sleep after the unexpected, unbearable journey home with James.

Next day Nick Corbett rang her at the office.

'I was just checking to see if you were back,' he said. 'Head all better now?'

'Yes, thanks. A few days by the sea did the head, and me, the world of good.'

'Are you free for dinner tonight?'

Oh, yes, she was free. Free as a bird. 'Yes, Nick.'

'Let's do something different. If you park behind the office I'll pick you up there. Seven-thirty?'

'Fine.'

Harriet returned to work feeling rather better. Nick was cheerful company, and right now she needed cheerful.

To enhance her sun-kissed look later she wore white linen trousers and camel silk sweater, and let her hair loose. She parked the car in the appointed place, and found Nick waiting for her, equally casual in jeans and the inevitable polo shirt.

'You look gorgeous,' he said, and kissed her cheek. 'You should always wear your hair like that.'

She shook her head. 'My clients would never take me seriously. Some of them had trouble in switching their accounts to a woman as it was when my predecessor left the firm. Where are we going?'

Nick gave her his most winning smile. 'I was too late to book anywhere so I ordered in. I thought a quiet evening at my place would be good.'

This was an invitation Harriet had so far steadfastly refused. But tonight the alternative was to go back to the Lodge with only herself for company, so she smiled in agreement.

Nick's flat was in one of the buildings near the market hall, with tall ceilings and big windows overlooking the town centre. 'They made such a good job of the renovation in this building it's worth the catastrophic price I paid for the flat,' he said as he showed her into his living room. 'What would you like to drink?'

'I'm driving, as usual, so something soft and harmless, please,' she said, a request that obviously disappointed Nick.

He was animated company as usual as he brought her

up to date with the latest gossip. The risotto was good, so was the inevitable tiramisu which followed it, and while Harriet kept to grapefruit juice topped up with lemonade Nick drank the expensive wine he'd obviously chosen with care.

He refused her help to clear away the meal, and came back with a coffee tray. 'So tell me, are the rumours true?' he asked.

'Rumours?'

'I heard on the grapevine that your father's getting married again.' His eyes gleamed as he joined her on his expensive leather chesterfield. 'He's been seeing a lot of the elegant Madeleine Fox lately. Are the rumours true?'

'I'm sure you'll soon know if they are,' she assured him, her pleasure in the evening, never more than lukewarm, instantly dispelled.

'If they do tie the knot he'll move into that fabulous manor house of hers, of course. And you'll be left alone, Harriet.' He moved closer. 'You don't have to be. I'd be only too delighted to keep you company at River House.'

Harriet stared at him blankly. 'What do you mean, exactly?'

He smiled eagerly. 'We've been seeing a lot of each other lately, so I think we should get married as soon as possible. My mother is always telling me it's time I had a wife, and you're the perfect choice, Harriet—'

'Why?'

Nick thrust a hand through his floppy fair hair, smile fading. 'What do you mean, why?'

'What makes me the perfect wife, Nick?'

'You're clever, attractive, and we get on well together.' He pulled her into his arms. 'And I bet we'd be dynamite in bed together too.' His groping hands were hot and damp through the silk sweater as he kissed her, but when he thrust his tongue in her mouth Harriet pushed him away and forced a cough.

'Sorry,' she croaked artistically. 'Can I have some water, please?'

Nick raced off to the kitchen and came back with a brimming glass. Harriet drank deeply, and then smiled ruefully at her host. 'I do apologise.'

'No problem,' he said shortly, though there obviously was from his point of view. There was a problem from hers, too, she realised, depressed. After James, kissing any other man was out of the question. Always had been.

'I really am sorry, Nick. I'm still not a hundred per cent.' Harriet put a dramatic hand to her head as though it ached. 'I think I'd better get myself home to bed.'

'I hoped you'd share mine tonight,' he said with one of his winning smiles.

'Yes, I gathered that. Sorry, Nick.'

'You could at least tell me what you think of my proposal before you go!'

Harriet looked at him levelly. 'You tell me something first, Nick. If my home was a flat here in town instead of River House, would you feel the same enthusiasm for me?'

He flushed angrily. 'That's not a very pleasant thing to say, Harriet.'

'You haven't answered my question, so let me put it another way. You took over from my father at the bank, so when you heard the marriage rumours about him perhaps you fancied taking his place at River House, too. And the only way to do that would be through marriage. With me.'

Nick's practised charm fell away from him like a discarded coat. 'Why the hell not?' he said arrogantly. 'You could do a lot worse than me, Harriet. There are plenty of women here in town who'd say yes in a flash if I proposed.'

'Then marry one of them,' she advised, and picked up

her bag. 'I'm afraid the answer's no. But thank you for asking—and for dinner. Goodnight.'

On the drive home Harriet was half inclined to confront her father immediately and ask if the rumours were accurate, but decided against it when she reached the Lodge. Her evening had been unsettling enough as it was. If she'd had the remotest idea about Nick's ambitions she would have turned the offer of dinner down flat before he got to his ridiculous proposal. She sighed heavily. Her self-esteem was taking quite a hammering these days. It was obvious now that Nick Corbett's sole reason for seeking her company these past few months had been to get a foot in at River House.

Harriet heard no more from James, other than news from Moira that at the moment he was too heavily involved with the expansion of his Live Wires Group for visits to the Old Rectory.

'Which is just as well, because now the plumbing's sorted—at astronomic expense—I think I'm coming down with flu. In the meantime I'm going stir-crazy. I hope we can get together soon for the lunch that never happened, Harriet.'

'We'll sort something out when you're better.'

'How are you now, Harriet? No more migraines?'

'No, indeed. Thanks to my holiday by the sea, I'm absolutely fine.'

This was pure fiction, but Harriet was sure that if she said it often enough it might become fact, and made a note to send get well flowers to Moira.

The Sunday lunch passed off with reasonable success, mainly because Harriet had warned her sisters in advance that their father had invited a friend to join them. Julia, of course, merely felt amused curiosity and, since Gervase was on hand to curb Sophie's jealous reaction to Madeleine Fox, the introductions passed off smoothly. The meal was not only superb, as usual, but a lot easier for Harriet because Margaret had volunteered to stay to serve the first two courses.

Conversation after the meal was easy enough, since Julia was perfectly happy to talk about the fashion shoot, details of which, happily, fascinated Sophie as much as Madeleine Fox. And because the lady was also interested in news of Annabel, happy at home with Pilar, Sophie thawed considerably, particularly when she learned that Madeleine lived at Fossedyke Court. Aubrey Wilde was happy in his guest's company, but not in an overt enough way to raise any suspicions, and though Harriet had fully expected a wedding announcement, the party broke up with only the usual thanks and an invitation from Madeleine to repeat the pleasure at her place soon. The minute Aubrey left to drive Madeleine home, Sophie pounced on Harriet.

'How long has this been going on with Mrs Fox?'

'I don't know. I've only just met her myself. Her golf handicap is only eight, so they have a lot in common.'

Julia smiled her cat-like smile. 'Not just golf, I fancy. Pa is definitely smitten.'

'Smitten?' said Sophie, horrified.

'Why not?' Gervase said calmly. 'Your father's a relatively young man, and Mrs Fox is an attractive woman.'

'Surely he doesn't want to bring her here to live!' Sophie turned on Harriet. 'You must know more about this than you're letting on—'

'She'll hardly want to move from Fossedyke Court,' interrupted Julia. 'I thought an old man lived there alone, Harriet.'

'He died and she's recently inherited it, so he was obviously a relative.' Harriet yawned. 'Does anyone want tea?'

'Actually, we need to get off,' Gervase warned his wife. 'Can't wear Pilar out now we know what life is like without her.'

'No, indeed,' agreed Sophie instantly. 'But don't forget to keep me in the picture about Mrs Fox, Harriet.'

Julia laughed. 'I suppose you want her to demand Pa's intentions!'

Harriet was surprised to find she enjoyed the evening alone with her sister after Sophie went, even when satisfying Julia's curiosity about the first event organised at River House.

'So come on, Cinderella, was the dress a success?'

Harriet laughed. 'It certainly was. Though I wouldn't have chosen something like that for myself.'

'Tell me something I don't know!' Julia smiled lazily. 'So more details, please. Who exactly hired the house?'

'James Crawford, head of the Live Wires Group, aka the unsuitable object of my teenage passion,' Harriet announced, and laughed when her sister's jaw dropped. 'Father's probably sorry that he made me dump James back then now he's so successful... There's the car. I'd better get going. What time will your people arrive tomorrow?'

'At eight and work through until at least six. I'll put my bedroom at the models' disposal. By the way, I asked Margaret if she fancied doing the catering during the shoot and she was all for it.'

Harriet's eyes lit up. 'What a brilliant idea, Julia. She won't be needed to clean the house while your lot are here. And now John's retired they can do with the extra money. What kind of food are you talking about?'

'I suggested something hearty and meaty, plus a vegetarian choice and salads, so she's going shopping first thing in the morning. I'll pay her when she comes back.'

Julia turned with a smile as Aubrey came in. 'You weren't long.'

He smiled genially. 'I thought I'd keep you company and let Harriet get to bed early, ready for work tomorrow. Though she works too hard, in my opinion.'

A good thing she did, Harriet reflected darkly as she got ready for bed. It gave her less time to worry. And right on cue, as if she'd conjured him up at the mere thought, James rang.

'How are you?'

'Better. Thank you.'

'I wasn't alluding to your migraine!'

'I'm perfectly fine otherwise, too,' she assured him.

'I'm not to be a father after all?'

'Not of any child of mine.'

Silence.

'Is that the truth, Harriet?'

'Yes,' she said tightly, fingers crossed.

'If I were there I'd know. You were never good at telling lies.'

'Why on earth would I lie about something like this?'

'That's obvious!'

'Not to me.'

'If you were expecting my child your father would have you married to me in a flash now my money's made me eligible. Eligible to him, at least, if not to—'

Harriet rammed her finger on the off button, and managed to put the phone down gently instead of hurling it across the room.

The next few days were so full there was no opportunity to dwell on personal problems. After hiring a car for the week to get into town, life was hectic in work but, because Julia would be the necessary family presence at River House, Harriet's watchful eye was unnecessary at home while an amazing amount of people took it over during the fashion shoot, which went off without a hitch. When it was all over, Charlotte handed over the cheque, minus her fee, Julia went straight back to London and Aubrey delayed his return home until Margaret had put the house to rights after the shoot.

'I hope this hasn't worn you out, Margaret,' said Harriet when it was all over.

'Good heavens, no. It was such fun being part of it, and everyone was complimentary about my cooking. John enjoyed working with me too.' Margaret smiled wryly. 'He's finding retirement a bit boring. He doesn't play golf like your dad, and our garden isn't huge, so he really likes helping out up here.'

'I could pay him to do that on a regular basis now if he likes,' offered Harriet.

'He'd be only too pleased.' Margaret frowned at Harriet as she burnished the gleaming counter tops. 'He could do the mowing for a start, which would save you doing it at weekends. I worry about you, Harriet.'

'Why?'

'Someone has to,' the woman said darkly. 'You'll be tired out after going down to Wales by train to fetch the car.'

'Not much option. I need transport.'

CHAPTER THIRTEEN

WHEN a television crew moved into River House to film a couple of scenes from a popular sitcom Harriet decided to ask Sophie if she fancied to driving over to watch. Her sister shrieked with delight, and promised to be there next morning after taking Annabel to nursery school.

'Pilar can pick her up—it's just wonderful to have her back, Harriet.'

'I hope you're paying her enough.'

'Gervase gave her a big rise and bought a new television for her room. And not just because she's so good with Annabel,' added Sophie hastily. 'We're really fond of her.'

Aubrey went off to stay at Fossedyke Court again before the television company invaded to take over the house, and Harriet's only option was to take more leave to maintain a watchful family presence. Two spare bedrooms were made available for the actors, but a catering truck was set up for meals this time round. Utterly fascinated by the cameras and lights and cables trailing everywhere on the ground floor of the house, Harriet kept out of the way in the hall to watch well-known faces at work, amazed by the extraordinary number of technical people needed to shoot the scenes.

Sophie arrived, dressed to the nines and buzzing with

excitement as she took in all the activity. 'Are they paying a lot of money?' she whispered to Harriet.

Harriet nodded. 'Enough to swell the River House business account and pay Margaret the extra she deserves to clear up afterwards.'

'Fabulous! Can we watch as they shoot an actual scene?'

To take advantage of the good weather, the outdoor scene was shot first. The sisters watched the proceedings together in fascination, Sophie delighted when they were invited to eat lunch with the crew.

'Great house you have here, Miss Wilde,' said the director. 'I'm Ashley Wade.'

'My sister, Sophie Barclay,' said Harriet, and Sophie beamed at him.

'This is all so fascinating! How long will you be here?'

'The weather should let us do all the outdoor stuff today, so with luck we should be finished by Friday at the latest.' He smiled at Harriet. 'You'll be glad to have the house to yourself again.'

'You didn't tell him you don't actually live there,' whispered Sophie as they went down to the Lodge afterwards.

'No need for him to know,' Harriet said.

'He's very attractive!'

'Is he?'

'Oh, *Harriet!* You're impossible. By the way, I've invited some friends to dinner on Saturday and I insist that you come too. Now don't say no. You'll feel flat once this lot go away so make the effort. I promise you'll like the people I've invited.'

Sophie was right. Once the film crew had departed with all its traffic and trailers the quiet was so intense by contrast Harriet was glad of an evening away from River House.

The weather was so warm Harriet drove her credit card

to town. She returned home later to a phone call from Moira, who thanked her for the flowers, reported that she was no longer infectious, and could Harriet manage lunch one day in the week to tell her all about the filming? There was no mention of James.

Harriet whiled away the rest of the afternoon by pampering herself. Tonight she would do Sophie proud. The creamy-pink linen shift she'd bought earlier was demure enough from the front, but cut lower in the back and shorter in the skirt than she would have preferred. It had been so pricey her only consolation was the matching jacket which meant it could be recycled for Lily's wedding later in the summer, along with the nude pumps bought for the party.

'My God, Harriet, you're a delight to the eye,' exclaimed Gervase, as he opened the door to her. 'Where's the car?'

'I parked it along the road for easy getaway.' She smiled as her sister appeared in a jade silk dress which had probably cost at least twice as much as Harriet's. 'Hi, Sophie.'

Her sister smiled in approval as she kissed her. 'That's new! I *love* the dress.'

Harriet flung out her arms as a small figure in a nightie came running down the stairs, with dark, pretty Pilar hot on her charge's heels.

'Auntie, I'm better now. Look, look! Pilar came back.'

Harriet swung Annabel up and kissed her soundly. 'So you are, and so she has. Hello there, Pilar.'

'Hola señora.' The girl smiled warmly, and held out her arms for Annabel. 'Come, I take you to bed.'

'I'll be up to read you a story as soon as the last guest arrives,' promised Sophie.

'I'll do that,' said Harriet quickly, and blew kisses to her beaming niece as Pilar took her upstairs. She followed Gervase and Sophie to join the guests in the big garden at the back of the house and accepted a glass of Pimms to sip during the introductions and greetings session.

'I'm Philip Mountford,' said a late arrival. 'Who are you, and what do you do, and if you live here in town why haven't I met you before?'

Harriet smiled politely. The man was good-looking, very much aware of it, and very much not her type. 'I'm Harriet Wilde, sister of your hostess, I'm an accountant and I don't live in Pennington.'

'Harriet,' said Gervase, joining them with a Pimms jug. 'Let me top up your glass.'

'No, thanks. I've had my quota. Long drive home, remember.'

'Stay the night this time! Annabel would love that.'

For once, as an alternative to the Lodge of a very empty River House, Harriet was tempted. 'Better not. Father's away over the weekend.'

Philip Mountford's eyes gleamed. 'Where do you live?' he asked.

'An hour away by car,' said Gervase, and took her hand. 'Excuse us, Mountford, our final guest has arrived by the sound of it.'

Sophie was all smiles as she ushered her companion out into the garden. 'I'll introduce you to everyone later, James. You know Harriet already, so I'll leave you in her capable hands.'

'Evening, Crawford,' said Gervase affably. 'Could you drink a Pimms, or shall I get you a beer?'

James's dark, lean elegance was a striking contrast to the florid good looks of Philip Mountford. Harriet's heart rapped against her ribs as he shook his host's hand, requested a beer and then turned to smile at her. 'You look very beautiful this evening, Miss Wilde. I was told to give you a message. Annabel is ready for her story.'

Sophie came rushing across to intercept her. 'I'll read to her, Harriet. You stay and talk to James.'

Harriet shook her head and put her glass down. 'I promised. See you later, James.' She walked away without haste, hoping her back view was worth the money she'd paid for it.

'One story only,' Sophie called after her. 'Dinner's almost ready.'

Annabel patted the bed beside her eagerly as Harriet entered the bedroom. 'You were a long time, Auntie.'

'Sorry, darling. Which story do you want?'

As soon as the short, but harrowing tale of a lost puppy restored to its owner ended Pilar came in, and Harriet kissed her little niece lovingly.

'Goodnight, darling. I'll see you again soon. Goodnight, Pilar.'

James was waiting at the foot of the stairs when Harriet went down. 'In case you've forgotten the way there, I'm ordered to escort you to the dining room,' he informed her.

Harriet smiled brightly as they crossed the shining expanse of hall floor. 'I didn't know you were coming tonight.'

He raised a sardonic eyebrow. 'Obviously. Or you wouldn't be here.'

'Wrong. My father's away and the television people who were filming at River House all week have finished, so the place felt a bit lonely after they'd gone.'

'Even though you don't actually live in it?'

'There you are,' said Sophie, beckoning to them. 'Come and sit down; the first course is on the way. I've put you between James and Philip,' she whispered to Harriet, 'so have fun.'

The wine, as always with Gervase, was lavish and because most of the guests knew each other well the conversation was easy and entertaining, and Harriet soon found she was enjoying herself far more than expected. The bittersweet pleasure of sitting close to James was marred only by the proximity of Philip Mountford, who seemed convinced she was there solely for his benefit and kept crowding her.

'Shall I pop him in the eye?' James whispered at one stage, and grinned as she stifled a giggle.

'If all else fails I'll ram my heel into his foot,' she murmured. 'This crab is delicious,' she said aloud.

'So are you,' James whispered in her ear.

Harriet stared at him wide-eyed, her colour rising as she realised Sophie was calling to her.

'I was just telling everyone about the filming at River House, Harriet.'

Harriet found herself suddenly the focus of everyone's attention. Questions were fired from all directions as she and Sophie described the experience. She shot an apologetic glance at her sister after a while. 'Sorry—we must be boring everyone.'

Sophie smiled with unusual benevolence. 'Of course we're not. It was fascinating. Who's next on the list, Harriet?'

'A cookery show is filming an episode there next.'

'You must be coining it in hand over fist,' said Philip with relish.

Gervase gave him a cold look. 'A bit personal, Mountford?'

Philip shrugged. 'No offence. Given the chance to swell my cash flow, a film crew could take my place over any time.'

'But you live in a modern monstrosity,' called someone. 'Who'd want to film there?'

'If it's the right kind of modern, they might,' said

Harriet, and turned to James in an effort to change the subject. 'How is your sister? Is she completely over her flu now?'

When everyone transferred to the garden for coffee later, James took Harriet firmly by the arm. 'This is where I make it clear to that jerk that you are not available.' He was as good as his word and kept so close to Harriet from then on that Sophie cast knowing glances at them from time to time, obviously convinced her matchmaking had been successful.

'I can hardly blame the man for trying,' said James at one point. 'You look ravishing tonight.'

'Why thank you, kind sir.'

He moved closer. 'Are we friends again?'

'Of course.' She sighed regretfully. 'But lovely though this is, I must be leaving soon.'

His grasp tightened. 'If you're returning to an empty house I'll follow you home.'

Harriet's heart leapt. 'It would mean far too long a drive back for you afterwards.'

He shook his head. 'I've done it before, remember.'

She did, vividly. 'It's very kind of you, but I wouldn't dream of putting you to so much trouble again. I'll be fine on my own!'

'Of course you will,' he said harshly, and to her dismay turned away to speak to someone else.

At that point the party ended for Harriet and, pleading her drive home as the reason, she took her leave. Sophie grasped her hand urgently as she said goodbye. 'Is Daddy staying with Mrs Fox again?'

'Yes.'

'Do you think they'll get married?'

'I don't know, Sophie.'

'You should get married, too, you know, whether Daddy

does or not.' Sophie surprised Harriet with a hug. 'I'm glad you came tonight. We Wilde girls must stick together.'

Harriet hadn't driven far before she regretted turning down James's escort. A swift, startling thunderstorm resulted in heavy rain, which made the journey slow going. When she finally turned up the dark, tree-lined drive to the house she was grateful for the security lights. Wind rustled through the dripping trees as she bolted from the car to the Lodge door. She fumbled as she tried to fit the key in the lock, then stiffened, her heart in her mouth at the sound of footsteps.

'Harriet?'

She let out a shaky breath as her father came into view, wielding a golf umbrella. 'Lord, you frightened me. I thought you were staying with Mrs Fox.'

'I was. But I asked Sophie to let me know when you left her party.' Aubrey's face looked tense under the security light. 'May I come in? Or would you prefer to come up to the house?'

'Let's get out of the rain.' For once Harriet was glad of company as she unlocked the Lodge door and switched on lights. 'Is something wrong?'

Her father put the umbrella in the porch and came into the room, looking very sober. 'I know it's late but I need to talk to you, so I'll get straight to the point. I've come to ask for your blessing, Harriet.'

Her eyes narrowed. 'Blessing?'

He nodded. 'Madeleine and I are getting married. Quite soon, in fact. At our age there's no point in hanging about.'

'Congratulations.' Harriet managed a smile. 'What are your plans exactly?'

'We'll live at Madeleine's place.' Aubrey smiled ruefully. 'So you can have River House all to yourself at last now you've found a way to make it pay.'

Harriet shook her head, depressed. 'Not feasible, I'm afraid. While the film people were here I used some of my annual leave to keep an eye on things, but I can't keep on doing that. Nor can I depend on the house being hired often enough to provide sufficient income if I gave up my job.' Suddenly it all seemed too much. 'There's only one thing for it. There'll be hell to pay with Julia and Sophie, but you'll just have to sell, Father.'

To her surprise, he looked relieved. 'I was hoping you'd say that. Your mother would be appalled if she knew you were devoting your life to River House. You need a husband and children and a less demanding home of your own, Harriet.'

Her eyes hardened. 'If you recall, you once put paid to my hopes in that direction!'

'Crawford's not the only man in the world, Harriet. Besides, back then I thought it was just one of those boy and girl things doomed to die a natural death.' He sighed. 'But the only thing that died was your relationship with me. Which I regret, deeply. Do you still care for him?'

Unfortunately, yes. 'I hadn't thought of him in years before he turned up to hire our house.'

'Then why the devil haven't you found someone else?' Aubrey demanded. 'You could have had any number of men in your life since if you'd wanted, Harriet, Nick Corbett for one. Instead, you channelled all your energies into your job and the house.'

She looked at him squarely. 'Actually, I recently decided that it was time I left you with the running of River House now I'd set the ball rolling with the hiring scheme, but if you're moving out to marry Mrs Fox that's obviously not on. You'd better put the house up for sale as soon as possible.' She smiled bleakly. 'But to soften the blow, will you try to find a buyer who wants the house as it is? I'd hate to see it turned into flats or a residential home.'

'I've already made a start on that. While you were away in Wales I had Hugh Ames from Combe Estates look over the house to give me a valuation.'

Her eyebrows rose. 'You have been busy. Am I allowed to ask how much?'

'Of course you are, child,' he said irritably, and gave her a sum which took her breath away.

'A tad optimistic! You'd be lucky to get that in the present property market.'

'That's what I thought, and refused to go any further until I'd discussed it with you. But Hugh got back to me to say a buyer had got wind of the sale and is willing to give me the asking price without quibbling.'

'Good heavens!' She started at him, amazed. 'In that case it must be someone plugged into the local grapevine. Who do you know with money like that?'

'Now don't bite my head off, but I'm afraid the buyer is James Crawford,' said Aubrey with reluctance, and held up his hand. 'Don't look like that. I haven't accepted the offer. I'm no keener on the idea than you are. So if you hate the thought of him living here I'll turn him down flat.'

Harriet felt winded. She sat down abruptly. 'So he's finally got his revenge on us both, good and proper.'

'It looks like it. Which is damned unfair on *you*. I was the one who did the damage.' He looked at her in appeal. 'I swear I wouldn't have had him arrested, Harriet. That was just sabre rattling. Just getting him away from you was enough.'

'At the time I believed you meant every word, which is why I never forgave you,' she said sadly. 'Not that it matters now. James can have the last laugh and good luck to him. By all means sell to him, Father. I would hate the thought of anyone at all living here, so it might as well be him as anyone else. Ask Hugh Ames to find me something in town. I'll see the kitchen shoot through, then give up my brief flirtation with the media and move out.'

Aubrey stood up and for the first time in years took Harriet in his arms and held her close. 'If I had the time over I would do things a lot differently.' He tipped her startled face up to his. 'But one thing you must believe. It was your mother I loved from the moment I met her, nothing to do with the house. For her it was a sacred legacy, but for me it was always a burden. This will probably alienate you from me for good, but the truth is, Harriet, I shall be glad to leave the place.'

'Fossedyke Court is no smaller!'

'But Madeleine and I will live in the Dower House there. We'll merely act as caretakers for the main house until one of her sons marries and takes over.'

For two weeks Harriet lived in a constant state of tension, expecting a gloating phone call from James which never happened. She met Moira for the much postponed lunch, but the main topics of conversation were the television invasions at River House and Lily's wedding.

Harriet smiled as they got up to leave. 'A good thing you're fit enough to go shopping for a wedding outfit, Moira. You look really well.'

'Which is more than can be said for you, Harriet! You look a bit dark under the eyes.'

'The kitchen shoot was a tad challenging. They practically dismantled the kitchen to film it, but they put it back again, thank heavens. This time my father volunteered to be on hand, so I didn't have to take time off to keep an eye on things.'

Her father's decision had been a surprise to Harriet, but

she had accepted his help gratefully, also Madeleine's, who not only joined Aubrey for the shoot, but pitched in with help for Margaret afterwards.

Now it was over, River House was immaculate and quiet, there was no further word from her father about the sale of the house, and Harriet made the life-altering discovery that she was not pregnant after all. It knocked her flat. It was too much trouble to get up and clean the Lodge on Saturday as she usually did, or to go into town and look over the flats Combe Estates had available. It was past noon before she showered and dressed, and for once left her hair to dry any way it wanted. As she went downstairs a car drew up outside. She ignored the loud knock on the door and stood very still. Perhaps if she kept very quiet whoever it was would go away.

'Harriet!' shouted a familiar voice. 'I know you're there. Open up.'

She pushed her damp hair from her face and went on leaden feet to open the door. James, so elegantly casual he made her feel ten times worse, eyed her in concern.

'What's wrong?'

'Wrong?' she echoed with sarcasm. 'What could possibly be wrong? Do come in. This will soon be yours anyway.' She turned on her heel and marched over to the window seat. 'Please sit—'

Before she could get there he picked her up and sat down with her on his lap on the sofa. 'Stop struggling,' he ordered. 'Just sit there and listen.'

'I refuse to listen! I've heard all I need to already,' she retorted, horrified to hear her voice breaking. 'Let me *up—*'

'No. You're going to stay where you are until I've had my say.'

'As if you hadn't had that already,' she snapped, and sniffed inelegantly. 'Are you happy now at last? Taking over my home for a party was only the start. To make your revenge complete, you had to buy it and evict me as well!' The tears she'd been holding back for days suddenly burst the floodgates and she sobbed like a lost child against James's chest.

He held her close and let her cry, one hand smoothing her hair until she grew quiet. 'You left out the bit about the snow,' he said at last.

Two reddened eyes stared up at him blankly. 'What snow?'

'The tragic heroine always gets turned out into the snow,' he pointed out.

Harriet bit her lip to control a hysterical giggle. 'It may be funny to you, James Crawford, but it's pretty serious for me.'

'It's pretty damned serious for me, too, believe me!'

She drew in a long, shuddering breath. 'So. Mr Crawford. How did you find out the house might be for sale?'

'My brother-in-law plays tennis with Hugh Ames and usually trounces him. When Ames beat Marcus for the first time he had a drink or three too many, and let fall the news that he had the sale of the century coming up because your father was getting married and moving out of River House. Marcus thought I should know, but soothed his legal scruples by confiding in Moira, knowing she would immediately give me the news.' His intent eyes locked with hers. 'I jumped in with the asking price so you could stay in your house, not move out of it, Harriet Sarah Wilde. Once the official papers are in my possession, I shall hand them over to you as a present so you can go back where you belong at last.'

Harriet stared up at him, utterly astounded. 'Why on earth would you do that?' she demanded, once she'd recovered the power of speech.

'Coals of fire,' he said promptly, and grinned. 'And I hate to think of you homeless out in the snow.'

Harriet knuckled the last of the tears from her eyes. 'Cut it out, James. You can't mean this.'

'I most certainly do. Once all the legal stuff was in train, and your father and I had signed everything, he asked me to spare him a few minutes in private. Although it was plainly agony for him to get the words out, he told me a very interesting story about getting you away from me by threatening me with the law if you refused to toe the line.'

'Father actually told you that!' Harriet thrust a hand through her tangled hair in wonder.

James nodded. 'So now I know why you broke my heart.' He held up a hand. 'No need to look so sceptical. It's the truth.'

'Good,' she said unevenly, 'because it broke mine to do it.' She began to cry again into his chest until James put his hand under her chin and looked into her swollen face.

'Stop it, Harriet, you're killing me. My idea was to make you happy, not miserable.'

'I'm not pregnant,' she blurted.

He frowned. 'I know. You told me.'

'I lied. At the time I thought I was, but a few days ago I found out I'm not.'

His eyes flared with exultant heat as he bent his head to kiss her. And suddenly there was nothing to cry about, only the bliss of his mouth on hers and the warmth of his caressing hands on the body that cried out for his touch. It was a long time before he raised his head so they could breathe.

'We could do something about that very soon,' he offered unsteadily, rubbing his cheek against hers. 'But first I'd like to clear up a few points about the deeds of the house.

I will hand them over to you with great pleasure, but there's a proviso. You get them on condition that you marry me.'

She drew back to look him in the eye. 'So you're actually mentioning marriage now, are you?'

'Yes.' He smiled crookedly. 'I apologise for the crack made previously. I'm only human, Harriet.'

Her chin lifted. 'Perhaps I should mention at this point that I've had a prior offer from Nick Corbett.'

James stiffened. 'He wants to marry you?'

She shook her head sadly. 'He wants to marry Miss Wilde and live at River House.'

'He can forget that!' James kissed her until she cried for mercy, and then threaded his hand through her hair to keep her face turned up to his. 'Let's get something clear, Harriet. My motives are different from Corbett's. I want to marry you for the simple reason that I love you—always have, always will. As far as I'm concerned, you can sell the house and we'll buy something else, or finish doing up the one I have now,' he promised and kissed her again. 'The important thing is to live together at last. The location is irrelevant.'

'You mean that?' Harriet's heart leapt when she saw from the look in his eyes that he did.

'But before we make decisions about that there's still something I need to know.' He grinned. 'And this time I won't use sex to get at the truth.'

'How disappointing!'

'Later for that,' he promised huskily. 'Tell me why you moved out of River House to live here in the Lodge.'

She heaved in an unsteady sigh. 'I couldn't forgive my father for threatening to ruin your life—and mine with it. But I'd promised my mother during her last illness that I would make sure proper care was taken of River House, so I only moved as far as the Lodge.'

'And you've held to that all these years?'

'Yes.'

'And I'm the one accused of revenge!' James rubbed his cheek against her. 'I'll take damned good care to keep in your good books from now on.' He kissed her swiftly, then drew back, his eyes questioning. 'But when I first suggested it back then you seemed happy to leave home to move in with me.'

'I was. At the time Father's finances were in good shape and he was still a long way from retirement. A teenage daughter's input was unnecessary.' Her heavy eyes locked with his. 'Not that I gave any of that a thought. For you I was ready to forget everything, even my promise to my mother.'

James held her cruelly tight. 'So all this time you've been doing penance for that. Right?'

'Partly,' she admitted breathlessly.

'It's time to stop now, Harriet. So what's your answer?'

'What's the question?'

'Are you going to marry me, woman?'

'Since you've used such powerful persuasion, how could I say no?' Harriet yawned suddenly.

'Are you tired, my darling?'

She nodded, utterly ravished by the endearment he'd never used before.

'Then you should be in bed,' James said firmly and picked her up.

Harriet smiled at him luminously. 'You should be in bed, too.'

He grinned, looking like the James she'd first met. 'If you mean yours, I'm in full agreement!' He paused at the sound of a car coming up the drive. 'Is that your father?'

She nodded.

James set her on her feet and kissed her. 'In that case,

before we get to the good part let's go up to the house. I need to ask your father for his daughter's hand in marriage. We don't need his permission, of course, but as a gesture to future harmony let's be magnanimous and ask for his blessing.'

* * * * *

ROMANCE

Roccanti's Marriage Revenge — Lynne Graham
The Devil and Miss Jones — Kate Walker
Sheikh Without a Heart — Sandra Marton
Savas's Wildcat — Anne McAllister
The Argentinian's Solace — Susan Stephens
A Wicked Persuasion — Catherine George
Girl on a Diamond Pedestal — Maisey Yates
The Theotokis Inheritance — Susanne James
The Good, the Bad and the Wild — Heidi Rice
The Ex Who Hired Her — Kate Hardy
A Bride for the Island Prince — Rebecca Winters
Pregnant with the Prince's Child — Raye Morgan
The Nanny and the Boss's Twins — Barbara McMahon
Once a Cowboy... — Patricia Thayer
Mr Right at the Wrong Time — Nikki Logan
When Chocolate Is Not Enough... — Nina Harrington
Sydney Harbour Hospital: Luca's Bad Girl — Amy Andrews
Falling for the Sheikh She Shouldn't — Fiona McArthur

HISTORICAL

Untamed Rogue, Scandalous Mistress — Bronwyn Scott
Honourable Doctor, Improper Arrangement — Mary Nichols
The Earl Plays With Fire — Isabelle Goddard
His Border Bride — Blythe Gifford

MEDICAL

Dr Cinderella's Midnight Fling — Kate Hardy
Brought Together by Baby — Margaret McDonagh
The Firebrand Who Unlocked His Heart — Anne Fraser
One Month to Become a Mum — Louisa George

0212 GEN STD HB

Mills & Boon® Large Print

March 2012

ROMANCE

HISTORICAL

MEDICAL

Mills & Boon® Hardback

April 2012

ROMANCE

A Deal at the Altar	Lynne Graham
Return of the Moralis Wife	Jacqueline Baird
Gianni's Pride	Kim Lawrence
Undone by his Touch	Annie West
The Legend of de Marco	Abby Green
Stepping out of the Shadows	Robyn Donald
Deserving of his Diamonds?	Melanie Milburne
Girl Behind the Scandalous Reputation	Michelle Conder
Redemption of a Hollywood Starlet	Kimberly Lang
Cracking the Dating Code	Kelly Hunter
The Cattle King's Bride	Margaret Way
Inherited: Expectant Cinderella	Myrna Mackenzie
The Man Who Saw Her Beauty	Michelle Douglas
The Last Real Cowboy	Donna Alward
New York's Finest Rebel	Trish Wylie
The Fiancée Fiasco	Jackie Braun
Sydney Harbour Hospital: Tom's Redemption	Fiona Lowe
Summer With A French Surgeon	Margaret Barker

HISTORICAL

Dangerous Lord, Innocent Governess	Christine Merrill
Captured for the Captain's Pleasure	Ann Lethbridge
Brushed by Scandal	Gail Whitiker
Lord Libertine	Gail Ranstrom

MEDICAL

Georgie's Big Greek Wedding?	Emily Forbes
The Nurse's Not-So-Secret Scandal	Wendy S. Marcus
Dr Right All Along	Joanna Neil
Doctor on Her Doorstep	Annie Claydon

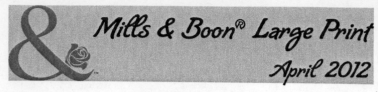

Mills & Boon® Large Print

April 2012

ROMANCE

Jewel in His Crown	Lynne Graham
The Man Every Woman Wants	Miranda Lee
Once a Ferrara Wife...	Sarah Morgan
Not Fit for a King?	Jane Porter
Snowbound with Her Hero	Rebecca Winters
Flirting with Italian	Liz Fielding
Firefighter Under the Mistletoe	Melissa McClone
The Tycoon Who Healed Her Heart	Melissa James

HISTORICAL

The Lady Forfeits	Carole Mortimer
Valiant Soldier, Beautiful Enemy	Diane Gaston
Winning the War Hero's Heart	Mary Nichols
Hostage Bride	Anne Herries

MEDICAL

Breaking Her No-Dates Rule	Emily Forbes
Waking Up With Dr Off-Limits	Amy Andrews
Tempted by Dr Daisy	Caroline Anderson
The Fiancée He Can't Forget	Caroline Anderson
A Cotswold Christmas Bride	Joanna Neil
All She Wants For Christmas	Annie Claydon